DAGMAR'S DAUGHTER

DAGMAR'S DAUGHTER

KIM ECHLIN

PENGUIN

VIKING

VIKING
Published by the Penguin Group
Penguin Books Canada Ltd, 10 Alcorn Avenue, Toronto, Ontario,
Canada M4V 3B2
Penguin Books Ltd, 27 Wrights Lane, London W8 5TZ, England
Penguin Putnam Inc., 375 Hudson Street, New York, New York 10014, U.S.A.
Penguin Books Australia Ltd, Ringwood, Victoria, Australia
Penguin Books (NZ) Ltd, cnr Rosedale and Airborne Roads, Albany,
Auckland 1310, New Zealand

Penguin Books Ltd, Registered Offices: Harmondsworth, Middlesex, England

First published 2001

1 3 5 7 9 10 8 6 4 2

Copyright © Kim A. Echlin 2001
Author representation: Westwood Creative Artists
94 Harbord Street, Toronto, Ontario M5S 1G6

Publishers note: This book is a work of fiction. Names, characters, places and
incidents either are the product of the author's imagination or are used
fictitiously, and any resemblance to actual persons living or dead, events, or
locales is entirely coincidental.

The author would like to acknowledge the support of the Canada Council.

Printed and bound in Canada on acid free paper ∞
Text design and typesetting by Ruthe Swern

Canadian Cataloguing in Publication Data
Echlin, Kim A., 1955–
Dagmar's daughter
ISBN 0-670-89102-9
I. Title.
PS8559.C45D33 2001   C813'.54   C00-931042-8
PR9199.3.E23D33 2001

Visit Penguin Canada's website at www.penguin.ca

for
Olivia and Sara

From the Great Above she opened her ear
to the Great Below.
From the Great Above the goddess opened her ear
to the Great Below.
From the Great Above Inanna opened her ear
to the Great Below.
Inanna abandoned heaven and earth
to descend to the underworld.

The Descent of Inanna
—Sumerian story, 2000 B.C.

There is geometry in the humming of the strings.
There is music in the spacings of the spheres.
Study the monochord.

—Pythagoras

PART ONE

THE
WHIRLING SOUTH
WIND ROSE

There. In the darkness a bony girl. She ties an oilskin pouch close to her waist and hides it under salvaged blue homespun. Her breasts leak milk and swell with pain. She dreams of cutting them off. The rest of her is hunched and thin. The skin under her eyes is smudged. She prepares to disappear into the hold of a ship heading down the coast to the gulf. She hides under a seine-gallows hung with newly barked nets. The sea crashes against the shore with neither joy nor remorse. Men's skulls down there. Poisoned fish. Torn and tangled nets of bad springs. The girl will stow away in the home boat's stale hold behind barrels of instruments. Now she waits.

Her name is Moll, though she was never baptized. The woman she called mother went silent before she was born. Her father was known as a fisherman, arms powerful as a machine. He sailed the great trawlers that swept the sea clean of fish. When he came back, men looked for him, asking, Where's buddy? They wanted spruce beer from his root cellar. They were his friends. When he got drunk he fought them and went to his daughter's bed.

Moll bore a blue baby, hardly knowing what was happening to her. She took it and tied it to a stone and dropped it into the sea. She was long-limbed and taller than any man in her village, too skeletal to show what everyone knew and didn't speak. She couldn't read. She signed herself into the world with drops of pee in a hole in the woods. This is her truth unconcealed. Even this will darken.

With the girl in its maw, the boat left the Labrador shore for the gulf. She took her father's eyestone and wore it in the oilskin pouch against her bottom rib. He would not notice it was gone until a summer and a fall and a winter had passed, and when he found out he cursed nature. By then Moll no longer feared death, for death and dying are the very life of the darkness.

A storm cracked Moll's ship in rough halves and everyone went down. She went down. She was whirled and spun below and divested of what she once was. Saltwater filled her mouth and throat and she became, in the lowest deep, a lower deep. There she achieved the silence that portends a new tongue. She came up again without hair and tied herself to a barrel of fiddles in the freezing salt waves. After two days and a night she washed up a blue meagre hag on the shore of a little island in the Gulf of the St. Lawrence called Millstone Nether.

Millstone Nether was a place first inhabited by rascals: merry-begots and hangashores, sleveens and slawmeens, some plain slackfisted, others eager to distract fate. From their couplings was born a settlement of people who subsisted on the sea's fish and the shallow soil's roots. There were many remote strips of land in the mouth of that great river, places that came and went with the tides and frail memory, places with poor harbours and treacherous shoals called by such names as Gulf Graveyard or Captain's Concern and never marked on the maps. Only a seaman who could rote the shore dared Millstone Nether's tricky western harbour, listening for the waves against hidden rocks. Off the northern tip was another tiny harbour, an hour's row on a civil sea to a remote and sparsely inhabited stretch of mainland.

Each of the islands in the gulf had its own nature, some better for hay, some for lumber, some for coal. Their mongrel languages were cobbled out of French and Gaelic and English and Montagnais. With time, pride came to the rascal-infested places and some islands claimed the best fishermen, some the best woodsmen. Millstone Nether's impractical claim for itself was music. Everyone there could play something or sing a ballad or dance a bit. Fishermen created a whistling language to talk between their lonely boats out at sea, and young girls clapped intricate rhythms invented from listening to the endlessly varied strophes of robins.

Sometimes ships went down off the north shore and barrels washed up from their splintered hulls. One year it was barrels of flour. In the year the people called the fat-spring, it was twelve barrels of whisky. But one miraculous year a barrel of fiddles in fancy cases blew up. And with it, another barrel full of whistles and guitars. There was even a double bass. The Millstone Nether people pulled up the barrels and dried everything out and tuned the instruments and taught themselves to play. They played in each other's kitchens and then they raised a simple pole house with a rind roof and a platform out in the woods beyond the settlement. On summer nights they lit ships' lanterns along the front of the platform and everyone came to play. There was laughter through those nights as they wove each other's riffs into their songs and pushed the music hard toward the silence that separates the rising from the falling measure.

One dry spring, everything brittle with thirst, the people of the settlement were having a time at the pole house. They drank plenty of beer and blueberry wine and played jigs and reels and sang. As night wearied on most of them left and those who stayed were too drunk to want to move. One small boy fell asleep by a lantern, left by his mother for his father to carry home. Hidden in the woods Moll bent over the bronze pot she had salvaged from the sea. She tapped its side and ran a heavy smoothed stick around its rim until the metal vibrated with moans and echoes. The musicians set down their fiddles and pocketed their spoons. Here was a sound they did not know. They had seen the traces her skeletal fingers and toes left along the shore and the waves washed away. She scavenged the woods and shore for things to eat. With nothing but her bony fingers she hollowed out holes where she hid stolen potatoes and spines of fish. She was indifferent to the people, her own bones and flesh more *prima materia* than woman. She was remote even to herself.

She set down her singing bowl and walked into the pole house among those who were left that night, all blind with drink. She stood over the beloved child sleeping on a pile of fragrant, dry pine needles, curled up beside a lantern, his eyes darting back and forth under fallen lids. Transparent as a sudden gale whipped up out on the sea, Moll kicked the lantern over. The child's sweater caught fire, then his trousers. The pine needles blazed skyward in a single wheeze and engulfed him in a little coffin of flame. Before he could awaken, his skin bubbled and his eyes melted back into his blackening skull.

No one saw her. No one at the pole house remembered anything. They had drunkenly beat out the fire and no one noticed the child was missing until dawn when they returned and pulled his bones out of the ashes.

Freak accident, they said, heads thick with remorse.

Sad-cruel, they answered, looking for elusive solace in their sighs. And they grew yet more hardened against ways that may not be questioned on an island in the sea.

Moll found the body of Meggie Dob's mother on the shore during the late fall storms, flesh bloated with saltwater, a strange open-mouthed fish caught between her legs. She ran her hands in consecration over the stretched and stinking purple skin, untwisted the flotsam from her hair and broke the chain of a locket from around her neck where the swelling skin had cut itself around the links. She dragged the heavy corpse far enough away from the sea's edge that the tide could not snatch it back. Then she walked down to the wharves. She loitered behind a spruce tree, and when a fisherman came ashore with his catch she stepped out and for the first time revealed herself. The man stared at the skeletal figure drawn to its full height before him. Tentatively he tossed a fish to her and she strode out and picked it up. While he watched, Moll squatted down, staring at him from her blank black eyes and ate it raw, spitting the long backbone into her tattered blue dress. She beckoned him to follow her. The fisherman left his catch open in his dory to the screaming gulls and walked behind her at a careful distance. By the time he saw the drowned body, Moll had disappeared into the shadows.

An early winter storm of swirling grey snow whipped the shores of Millstone Nether that night and froze the windows of the room where the women huddled around Meggie Dob and her water-bloated mother in a pine box with its lid nailed shut. They repeated to each other what the fisherman had said about the bony woman who appeared out of the woods. Listening to the pinging of ice on the thin panes, they wondered how a woman could survive winter abroad, and they commissioned the men to build Moll a hut at the far edge of the settlement and to leave its door open for her. This was accomplished and though no one ever saw her during the short days, bits of spat-out bones appeared in a pile by the front door, and the skull of a whale and the rib cage of a harp seal appeared lopsided on each side of the door. All winter the misshapen body of a swile-head codfish hung frozen over the frame, lumpy at its crown where a larger fish had bitten but not killed it and the skin and scales had grown back in disorder. Later when spring warmth thawed it out, the flesh and scales drooped and stank and fell to the ground, leaving only the skeleton like a bit of coarse lace. The door opened and closed below it and the continuous round of day and night prevailed.

Far away from Millstone Nether, Norea Nolan was thirteen years old when she talked to a passing tinker one afternoon outside the village pub in her little town on the west coast of Ireland. The next morning she woke up to find her boots gone. She knew who took them, three tin-faced Catholic women with noses like crones'. It was the custom when Norea was a girl to take young girls' shoes and to bury them secretly out in the fields under rough piles of stones so the girls couldn't run away. Norea was the eldest of eight and the only girl.

Her village was on the edge of the sea, a worn quilt of land laid out in uneven squares. Against the crooked stone fences thin cows and scraps of sheep huddled away from the cold winds and drizzle. A girl could never find her shoes out there under stained curtains of rain. Now Norea had to go barefoot. She grew reedy and competent, helping her mother, Dagmar, watching the cycle of pregnancies and births, sharing with her in that house full of boys a narrow life of secret glances and bedtime caresses after all the work was done, more like a sister than a daughter.

Norea had just turned seventeen and her mother lay bleeding after giving birth to her last son. The midwife caught the baby, the placenta and then something that shone dull purple, the limp bloody flesh of a woman's worn-out uterus. The midwife did not know what it was and set her jaw at the sight of it. If it didn't belong outside, she thought, it must belong in, and she pushed it back but she couldn't stop the blood. Norea's mother pulled her frightened daughter's ear to her white lips.

Child, she whispered, tears falling from her eyes. Don't cry. *Tá mé sásta le m'staid.* I'm a bird with a broken wing. Carry me away on your shoulder. You can do better than I did. Promise me. Take me away from here.

Drinking and telling stories, they kept the body in the front room three days and nights and Norea had plenty of time to think. Before they moved the coffin from the house to the churchyard to bury her mother, Norea had a fit in front of her brothers, her father and the priest, in front of the neighbour women who'd scrubbed and dressed the corpse and now took turns keening for the dead and tending the motherless newborn. Sinewy of spirit, Norea stood at the end of the coffin and screamed, Leave me alone with her, leave me alone!

She tossed her long red hair and wept so bitterly that the young priest took everyone away and closed the door, murmuring, Give her a moment, then. Her only mother, and her now left to cope.

It was the first time in her life Norea had been alone in a room. Quick as she could and wailing loud enough to cover up any noise, she reached into the coffin and took the boots right off her mother's stiff still feet. She tied them under her skirt against her legs, closed down the lid and lay on top of the coffin, sobbing. Finally the priest pushed in, took the girl by the shoulders and nodded at the men to carry the coffin away without another look inside.

After the funeral, when half the village men lay drunk in her kitchen and the other half sat drunk in the pub, Norea wandered down to watch the seals popping their heads out of the waves. Her brothers were huddled like puppies in two big beds at home, but there wasn't a thing she could do. She reached under her skirt, pulled out her mother's boots and walked away. She walked as far as Dublin, pressing herself behind stone fences like a sheep during the day and feeling for the edge of the road with her feet at night. She talked to her mother-the-bird on her shoulder as she walked. She said hurried rosaries when she passed the roadside Mary shrines. When she arrived weary in the city, she saw tall buildings for the first time and couldn't imagine why people liked to live in such high rooms. She was afraid of being found and taken back, so she cut her hair and stole some trousers, called herself Pippin and got onto a ship as a scullery boy. She carried her mother across the sea farther than she'd ever imagined, and after she was discovered she spent the rest of her journey in the fearsome stench-filled hold, starving and filthy and thirsty and heartsick. Finally after twenty-eight days they sailed into the mouth of a great river that cuts half a continent in two.

The sea tosses up our losses, the torn seine, the broken oar. Norea saw the smoke of the settlement when they were anchored off Millstone Nether and jumped ship without a coin in her pocket, too afraid of what might happen to her if she stayed aboard. There was work trenching potatoes and minding children for a girl with strong arms, and for a while Norea slept in others' huts, under others' stairs. Still, she had no desire to live indentured, little better than what she'd left behind. Before four seasons passed she managed to save enough to buy a horse and cart, and each morning before dawn she milked the cows at Meggie Dob's farm and bought the milk, and to the satisfaction of those hard-working island women, she delivered milk and eggs and gossip through the half doors of the settlement, driving her milk wagon along and playing a little pennywhistle.

Is the milk fresh today? one teased.

If it were any fresher, it'd be grass, laughed Norea, handing over the clinking bottles.

Norea, called another, Finn said he had eggs cheaper than yours.

Watch out for that one, she flung back. He'll steal the skin off your bones.

Old Mrs. Murphy observed the cheeky red-haired, hard-working milk-girl and one morning sent her son Rory out to fetch the milk. He stood holding the empty bottles, tossing stones against a tree. He watched her drive her horse and admired how she swung down off the seat of her wagon, tied the reins and carried the heavy milk bottles, singing,

> The gardener's son being standing by,
> Three gifts he gave to me, me—
> The pink, the rue, the violet blue,
> And the red, red rosy tree,
> The red, red rosy tree.
>
> Come all you maids, where'er you be,
> That flourish in your prime, prime.
> Be wise, beware, keep free from care,
> Let no man steal your thyme, thyme,
> Let no man steal your thyme.

When he stepped in front of her she said, What's a young man doing standing about on a morning when the boats are already gone?

He laughed. I've been sent, he said.

And are you compelled?

Well, I don't know about that. How much for the milk?

Norea scoffed, What would you know about paying for milk? Your mother does all that. Then she handed him the full bottles, took the empty ones and drove her horse away.

Each morning Rory Murphy stood waiting for Norea.

Don't you ever work? she said.

Only after you've gone, he said. I could get to work earlier if you married me.

And what do you do in the evenings?

I sing with my mother.

Is that a fact?

I have my own house and a good bawn and a dory.

With his charming smile he sang, For in my mind, of all mankind, I love but you alone, and as she drove off, the melody of "The Nutbrown Maid" got tangled into the clop of her horse's hooves. All day and all night she thought and the next morning she agreed to marry Rory Murphy on the condition that she keep her own name and not give up her milk route. She hadn't walked across Ireland at night eating nettles to hand herself over to the first tuneful boy who came along. They moved into his house and Norea set to the task of learning to salt fish, and though she had no gift for it she planted carrots and potatoes in rows in the field out behind and coaxed things to grow.

On long summer evenings Norea and Rory took their supper to eat under the single apple tree beside the house. She sang to him in her mother tongue to tease him.

What's that? asked Rory, who'd never been off the island and was pleased by his bride's exotic stories from across the sea.

Let's get some sleep, said Norea.

You don't want to sleep, said Rory, slipping his hand under her blouse. What's that song?

Not out here, creatures can see, said Norea, pulling his hand away. Will you come straight to bed with me if I tell?

I'd come anyway.

It's the "Hauling Home" song. A month after the wedding the village makes a procession to the groom's house. The bride rides on a horse and there's a piper at the front door playing hard. When the groom gets there he sings a song, *Oro, 'sé do bheatha a bhaile, is fearr liom tu ná, céad bo bainne.* Then all the men get drunk.

And what does it mean?

It means, Welcome home, I'd rather have you than a hundred milch cows, she said, spitting out apple seeds.

He laughed. Do you miss home?

She looked back at him and lied, Not a bit. Then she added, I'd rather have you and a hundred cows.

They sat, hands touching in the easy contentment of lovers who have not yet quarrelled, enjoying evening as if it would never turn into night.

Eight months later cheerful Rory died in the great flu epidemic. Norea, with a child soon to be born, crawled into bed with him to warm his chills and sponge his feverish lips. He stirred one last time, reaching for her, and her tears fell over his cheeks and stained his face pink as if he were not dying.

The Millstone Nether women shook their heads, saying they'd never seen a corpse's face keep its colour the way Rory's did. After that Norea was careful where she let her tears fall. But not careful enough.

After the funeral, Norea trenched her potatoes. As she bent over the earth, a locket without a chain was tossed

across the rows, and landed by her feet. She picked it up out of
the caplin fertilizer and opened it and saw a picture of Meggie
Dob's mother inside. Through the bushes she glimpsed Moll's
naked, bony feet, dirt caked under her toenails. Norea
approached her and looked into Moll's blank black eyes.

It's yours from the sea, said Norea, holding the tossed
locket back toward her.

Sss eee! hissed Moll. She slapped her thigh and bit her lip.

Her eyes are open, Norea thought, but their sense is shut.
Then she said to the bony woman, Naught's anyone's in the
eyes of the sea.

Moll crouched back behind the bushes half-turned from
the outstretched hand, but Norea stayed still and through the
leaves she listened to Moll's lips forming sounds from moans,
Naaaw. Aye, sss eee.

After that Norea told little stories aloud to keep the rustle
in the bushes company. About the seals at home. About village life across the ocean. When she couldn't think of anything to say she'd sing in her ragged way. If Moll groaned
unseen, Norea groaned softly to keep her company. She
restored Moll's eloquence. To Moll's soul-alone solitude
Norea offered words in the wind.

Scarce half Moll seemed to live, dead more than half. In the
daylight she revealed herself in silent watching and hurling
stones. Men who drank said they went to her at night. They
bragged that her appetites were voracious and insatiable.
They told tales to each other of being wrapped in her dire
arms and of her legs twisted in a double knot around their
backs. They whispered about going at her until they were

half-dead of exhaustion and still she wanted more. They admitted of their backs being rained on with stones when they left and they lifted their shirts to show each other the bruises.

She'll devour you, they dared each other.

Moll sat on gaunt haunches, her strong hands sifting through fishbones and hoarded roots. She was never seen to sleep but seemed ever somnolent. Her blank black eyes were ringed and her sullen skin weather riddled. Norea told the women to leave a jug of milk or the heel of a loaf near Moll's door. When there was no more hope for the sickest of the sick the women visited Moll with kettles of boiling water. Moll told strange tales and chanted as she rendered out the insides of a pig and made ointment for limbs that might fall off. She made tea of sheep manure or dogwood berries for vomiting, cut off the sap bubbles of fir balsam and squeezed it into festering wounds. These were common remedies in those days that all women knew, but when nothing worked they still came to Moll. Sometimes with her the sick got better.

They found out when a boy got a fish hook caught in his eye. Though they were able to ease the barbs out of the flesh, the eyeball wouldn't heal and it seemed to the women a shard of metal was stuck in there. They took him to Moll. Her eyestone was the size of a pea, the colour of flesh, with a black speck in the centre of its whorl. Some thought it was the cutoff tip of conch shell from deep in the ocean. It was a living thing and had to be fed. Moll kept it in a bowl of sugar and rinsed it in a weak solution of vinegar before she dropped it into the eye of the frightened boy. It ate whatever was in there and saved his sight.

Moll had her uses and the people of Millstone Nether abided her much as they abided the sea that fed them and destroyed them with equal indifference. There is a certain darkness that bids us turn away. Moll's was this. It is the shadow in which the snake swallows a crying frog alive, the wolf eats the wing off a living duck frozen into the ice, the caribou drags a cancerous growth, falling and struggling up and falling again. These are the incomprehensible things that we encounter with a hand over the mouth and the eyes averted. Moll walked the inroad of old darkness, appeared and disappeared in an unpredictable way. And though the people did not attempt anything against her, they taught their children to fear her. They turned their eyes from her because what she was they feared to contemplate. They never spoke of her or when they did it was in fearful or ignorant ways. In the lower deep she had been divested of compassion and of all human desire save her own endless suffering. There would always be those drawn to her. Some would survive and some would not. One day a girl would be drawn to her dark music, a girl who did not fear to open her ear to the great below, a girl who did not fear the silence from which all music comes.

Each month Meggie Dob, who desired a child, cried at the coming of her blood. Norea, round with her own child, came to give Meggie back her mother's locket and found her weeping in the barn near the old bull. At Meggie's sadness, Norea couldn't help letting a few of her own salt tears fall into the straw. She used the same comfort words her mother-the-bird had often spoken, Don't you mind your troubles; something always comes of them. And she was careless how she let her tears fall.

The next day when Meggie went out to the barn she heard the cries of two babies from beside the old bull. She dug into the straw and found an infant boy tucked beside the coarse hair of the animal and an infant girl lying head to foot with him. She picked up the babies, swaddled them in her own soft sweater, and since no one knew where they were from, the people of the settlement agreed that Meggie Dob might keep them and raise them as her own. Meggie clasped Norea who came to visit and to bless the soles of the babies' tiny feet. The boy's eyes were fierce and his cry demanding. He was perfectly formed, already long limbed and strong. The girl was not. She had a slope to her shoulders and her tiny chin was stuck down on her chest. She had rocker-bottom feet, and a webbed neck and elbows. Her eyes were lit bright.

Meggie said to Norea, jostling the two of them at once, It's as if you cried them right out for me!

Irritable with her own baby's bumping inside against her ribs and bladder, Norea answered sharply, You must be hagged to say a thing like that!

But with a quick change of heart she hugged Meggie, arms full of those long-desired babies, and said, I don't know how they got here, but it's cruel wonderful for you. What will you name them?

Donal is the boy, Meggie said. Though he comes from tears, he will one day be world mighty. And this poor little fish will be Madeleine, after my own mother who drowned under the sea.

Norea gave birth at home alone and watched over her stubborn-jawed newborn with fierce resignation and the clear conviction that she would lose this daughter as she'd lost everyone she loved. When the child lived past a year, Norea finally believed she might survive and named her Dagmar.

Dagmar grew sturdy and strong and Norea let her do as she liked. She dropped her from the milk wagon at the little school each morning but the child always ran home early to watch the planting and picking. One day Norea gave her three carrot tops to root in shallow dishes of water on the windowsill. The next day the child's carrots had roots spilling in white tangles down to the floor. The little girl carried them outside and planted them near the house. That evening she solemnly dug up three well-formed carrots and gave them to Norea.

And where did you get these? said Norea.

I grew them from the tops you gave me, answered Dagmar.

Norea had no reason to disbelieve her. Instead she chopped off three more tops, handed them back to the child and watched with amazement as she repeated the miraculous growing of the day before. Then she gave her daughter apple seeds and watched a small orchard appear in twenty-eight days.

Norea studied her unnatural child and concluded that a bit of soil from this new country had got into her to make an unnatural species. Norea would have quietly contented herself with her daughter's crops of carrots, tomatoes and apples, but little Dagmar couldn't stop, and cleared larger sections of garden into the black spruce and tamarack, made a cold frame, and when she was older, she built the island's first greenhouse. Roots she sowed overnight—onions, potatoes—and the above-ground squashes and cucumbers she let take a little longer. There was enough to give away during the thin springs. Only once Norea said, Do you know how you do it?

The girl looked at her. It is easy. Plants want to live.

Norea then knew that her daughter grasped her uncanny power. She tried to teach Dagmar to speak Irish. But she refused and kept to the language of Millstone Nether. Exchanging seeds and looks and words, the girl and the young woman created a life in their small rooms filled with mysteries neither understood. Each night they lay side by side in bed, Norea soothing her daughter with stories and fingers laced through the child's.

Dagmar stuck her feet up in the air, grabbed her young mother's muscular thigh and teased, I've got your leg.

Norea wrapped her hand around the child's foot and said, I've got your toes.

The girl slipped away, scrambled down to the bottom of the bed and snatched at Norea's toes saying, No you don't, I've got yours.

Then she tipped off the bed and hid underneath, calling, Come find me! Before Norea could look, Dagmar appeared from under the other side, dragging out a pair of old boots, and asked, What're these?

Those are my mother's boots, said Norea as the girl put them on and shuffled along the floor. Hide them away again when you're done. They'll be yours when you're old enough, though you'll never need them. I'll see to that, and that's a promise.

Norea was only twenty, but she had travelled an ocean and married and buried a man and given birth to a daughter. There were still appetites. When her daughter was asleep at night, Norea sometimes stole out to meet a fisherman whose wife with five children was too tired for him in her bed. That was how, under an overturned dory, Norea got pregnant with a child she feared the island people would not abide. She decided she wouldn't carry a child whose father did not want to be known.

That droughty spring dry weather threatened all the meagre crops. Small forest birds, foxy-Toms and striped-heads and mopes and purple finches, kept flying against the settlement's windows. Norea and Dagmar got up at dawn and found them lying, necks broken on the ground, and gathered them up. Together they examined the coloured feathers, the staring eyes, the stiff, still feet. Norea delighted in watching the sun come up behind her daughter's curly dark hair falling over the dead birds. Dagmar examined the airiness of each wing, touched through the feathers into the birds' fine bones across their breasts. Mother and daughter dug little graves at the back of their farm, a row of bird-filled mounds to remind them of this hard dry spring of strange winds. Together they tore bright strips of rags and hung them against the windows of the houses to warn the birds away from their own reflections. When the work was done, Norea held young Dagmar's face between her large palms and tried to memorize the brightness of her eyes. She wrapped her gaze around this beloved one and worried about what to do about the baby she did not want.

As she pondered, she walked out in the field with Dagmar's hand in hers, looked at the parched apple trees and said distractedly, If we don't get some rain soon there'll be no apples this year. Dagmar stared gravely into the sky. Smurry clouds moved in from the horizon and a great rainstorm soaked the island with fresh water for two days and a night. When it was over they watched the fragrant apple blossoms open before their eyes.

Later in that month of odd weather, Norea remarked, It's hot for the wild strawberries this year, and the child said, Don't worry. Something will come of it.

By evening the temperatures had dropped and the low plants on their farm were thick with delicate fruit. After that, Norea tempered what she said about the weather in front of the girl. It was one thing to have a green thumb and another to reshape the sky. Norea watched her free-hearted daughter as if she were a foreign creature and she said to her, You won't have to run away as I did. All this place is yours when I turn into honey. She marvelled at the girl's strong mind and averted her eyes when Dagmar planted. It was better not to look, for she sometimes thought she saw new shoots and leaves growing right out of the girl's fingers.

Norea nudged the old fishbones away from the path up to Moll's door with her foot. She knocked and when no one answered she pushed it open.

Moll was crouched on the floor inside and said, What do you want?

Norea said, I need to get rid of something.

Moll looked up with blank black eyes. She said, Best babies are merry-begots.

I can't bear this child. These island people.

Tuck it in a basket, leave it at da's door. No one has a proper place but makes their own.

He'll never claim it.

Won't know breath your way.

Please.

Moll stood to her full height and said, Bring me boiling water.

Norea walked back to her house and put the kettle on. She took Dagmar to Meggie's house and asked her to watch the child overnight. She went back for the water and talked aloud. Rory, she said into the steam from the kettle, if you'd stayed I wouldn't be at this. She heard the kettle's whistle and quickly, to prevent the churning of her own thought, she took the boiling water back to the little shack where Moll crouched, sifting through a basket of sweet-smelling blossoms on the floor. Moll poured out a cup of water, snapped off some of the tansy flowers, stems and leaves, and mixed them in. She waved Norea over to a heap of old rags in the corner and handed her the tea.

Bitter buttons for the path wanderer, Moll said. Do not sorrow when what you lose you'll never have again.

Norea raised the cup to her lips and drank the hot sweet-smelling liquid. She swallowed and drank again and swallowed until it was all gone and then she waited. The poison spread warm and violent through her body, and terrified she put her fingers into her mouth and tried to get rid of what was not yet down. Her skin beaded in sweat and cramps roiled up from her stomach against her heart and down into her womb. She bent over herself as if she were going to die, then threw up to the side and fell back from the knotting pain that twisted from her insides out. She lay back panting and faint. Then the blood. She did not at first notice it. She was throwing up yellow froth, and desperately she turned on her hands and knees and sagged into a crawling creature. Her head dropped through the sweat and she saw blood between her legs and felt the wrenching at her womb and the cramps that seized her. Moll's cold hand pulled off her underthings. She fell on her elbows, cheek flat against the foul rags and begged for mercy from sour dry lips, but still the cramps waved through her body and still her insides heaved and the blood poured out of her until she fell limp into the floor.

In her delirium she saw all that she had been and what she would become. She saw seals and snow. She saw her own mother balancing on bird feet and broken wings. She saw Rory's lips singing and Dagmar's lips latching on to her swollen nipple. She saw Moll's bones.

Moll looked dispassionate at the colour of her skin and her swollen tongue and her lifeless closed eyelids. Moll listened to her moaning and mumbling, My belly, my back. She listened and then she went to her hole lined with blackberry earth up on the gaze for the night.

On the second afternoon Meggie Dob came by looking for Norea and Moll threw rocks at her to keep her away. Meggie pushed in and saw Norea lying in a filthy bloody heap on the rags.

What have you done to her? she demanded of Moll.

What have flowers done? What has dory's darkness done? Do not ask why! hurled back the bony woman squatting in the shadows between Norea and the door. Throw her in the sea. She's not needed here.

Stop! screamed Meggie. She pushed past Moll and sat by Norea's head and wiped her brow and commanded, Bring me water.

Moll brought her a bucket of water and Meggie wiped the blood and vomit from the limp woman and moistened her lips. She held her head in her lap and stroked her face and said, Norea, you can't die. Your Dagmar is crying. Where is her mother?

The young woman's lips opened, her eyes still shut. For three days and nights Meggie and the other women in the settlement took turns sitting with Norea in Moll's shack, opening her lips and feeding her milk and soup and molasses tea, cleaning her when she threw up again, dampening her tongue, rubbing her arms and legs, stroking her hair. Finally, the poison worked its way through her blood and sinews, and Norea mumbled, then moved a finger, a toe, asked for her daughter. Two things the poison changed. It took away the child. It rendered Norea fully and forever blind.

When she could finally stand to go home, she could not find her way alone but had to be led.

From that day Norea lived excluded from light, whether it was day's noon or a full-moon night. She caressed Dagmar's face with her searching fingers and was afraid to cry. She commissioned the child to lead her around the house, over and over, counting the steps, memorizing the corners. When she accomplished the house, they began on the bawn out back. They laid stones for her to tap her way along the edges of the gardens, to the greenhouse and back. Norea taught Dagmar to place everything where she could find it again. She arranged the bottles in the milk wagon and took Dagmar with her until she was sure the old horse would follow his route and bring her home. The women came out of their houses shyly in the early dawn to collect their bottles. At first they pitied her but Norea began her joking. Can't see for looking, she said. You're a pretty sight today, just out of bed! She teased them until the women forgot that she was blind. Norea memorized the shape of the island with the soles of her feet. She memorized the winds in their seasons and the smell of each household. She could soon walk anywhere with her little cane, laughing in her old way, disguising her blindness. She used her finger inside her teacup to pour tea for friends and got an accurate ear for their voices and a good nose for their odours like a creature who lives underground. People stopped thinking of her with either shyness or pity; there were other things to worry over. And though Norea never said a word against Moll, the people of Millstone Nether were once again wary of the bony woman and stopped taking their sick to her.

But Moll would not be set aside. She appeared on the shore, waiting for fish when the boats came in. She crouched in the shadows of the pole house listening when the people gathered for music. She pressed her smudged face up against the panes of the greenhouse when young Dagmar worked alone. But if Norea heard her rustling in the bushes as she worked the gardens with her daughter, she said, Don't worry, Dagmar. She doesn't want you, only what you may become.

The fabled music of Millstone Nether had a well-defined centre but no clear circumference. The best of the island's musicians had a capacity like the sea's to find the single note in the vastness and to give it birth, shaping it into a life of scenes and inflections, pauses and climaxes, and finally allowing it to sink back into the currents whence it came, music heard so deeply that it is not heard at all.

Donal Dob and his best friend, Colin Cane, were like any of the island boys, jigging in the summer and hopping icebergs in the winter. They heard Millstone Nether's music in their cradles and picked up their first instruments young. Donal clambered up on a stool at a kitchen party, wrapped one small hand around the long neck of a double bass, grasped a bow in his fist and sawed out his first sounds. He begged Meggie to find a bass for him and she did. The boy was fascinated by the instrument's low sounds—especially the C string—as he had never been equally engaged by a human voice. He played its highs and lows, searched its range and potency. Up on the three-legged stool in the kitchen at home, hands stretched, bow held firmly, he played his double bass for his mother and sister. His instrument made him feel he could fill up a room. He strengthened and stretched his hands to caress and thrum out single notes and thick chords. More and more he recognized himself in the striding glissandos of his bass's majesty, the darting dark notes of its lover's dance, the athletic shapes of its light-footed, pleasure-loving young man.

Colin Cane's parents had died young, when their boat was tossed against the rocks in a sudden storm. There were no photographs of them. His relatives cleared out their rooms and gave young Colin his family's old fiddle, a guitar and the broken-down piano. Colin could get a tune out of any instrument that was lying around and always carried a pair of spoons in his pocket. He played to be part of whatever house in the settlement he was staying at until he was finally old enough to return to his parents' house alone. He scratched away on the fiddle because he was sure he could hear his mother's sweet voice in it, and he thumped on the old piano, listening for his father's beat and caress. His disposition was like a wave's, by turns calm and turbulent, still and still moving. Resigned young to all change, he had a natural pliability that let him move around the rocks and shoals that were too great to shape differently. When he played the music of Millstone Nether as the old people did, he was soothed against adversity and he took the traditional tunes for his own and strung them together in medleys. There wasn't a musician on the island who couldn't play along with Colin, so familiar were his songs.

But his friend Donal Dob was more like the red rock cliffs rising over the north end of the island, carved by wind and waves into craggy shapes that pleased the eye with their changing shadows and reflected light. He was rarely at ease in the traditional music. He worked harder than Colin did at playing the exact sounds and rhythms he heard and he was much admired by other musicians for his youthful mastery. He never felt satisfied, but he too always returned to the traditional notes, yearning to believe that somewhere at their unconquerable core—if he only searched hard enough—was the key to his restlessness. He did not understand that he was searching not for music but for virtuosity. As he grew older he believed that his fate did not lie in the reels and strathspeys of Millstone Nether but in music that came from away.

Madeleine Dob, with her little tucked chin and her sloped shoulders and her webbed elbows, did not grow tall. She collected blueberries and squashed them and painted pictures of blue cows with a frayed stick on the stalls of her mother's barn. When blueberry season was over she visited Norea and asked for beets to make a deep red. She wouldn't stop painting red and blue pictures.

Well, said Meggie Dob to the child, you've found your two ardours.

What does that mean?

I mean red for fire and blue for love—it all comes back to that.

But I want different colours.

That winter Meggie bought colour for the girl and soon she covered every surface of her mother's small house on stilts with her flat pictures. She recast the sights of Millstone Nether: skating parties and summer bonfires and trenching potatoes and men dragging nets off boats. She gave each drawing a strange title and painted the words into her borders. On her picture of a man being blown off a ship she wove into the border *Happy-Go-Lucky* and on a scene of a bawn filled with goats she wrote *Purple Cow Lost*.

If there were ever a conflict between instinct and consciousness in her choices of what to paint and how, instinct won out. Her dogs flew and her winter trees were laden with fruit. There were fish in the clouds and babies under the sea. She couldn't say why. Once, when asked why she drew a two-faced head, she said, I didn't have two pieces of paper.

Though Madeleine was not pretty, Meggie always said to her, Your eyes are lit with a full moon's light; that's beauty enough for anyone. She kept finding paints and paper for her foundling daughter and gave her empty tins for her brushes and set up a table by the window of their tiny house and let her fill her lonely girlhood with those eerily bright flat pictures.

It was a young island where art and life went hand in hand. Women wove mats for their floors with the things ready at hand, men carved a bit of an idea into a branch for a walking stick. On the island it was thought that life could not be beautiful without art, nor art flourish without life, and so, whenever there was extra time or material around, something prettying was made. But Madeleine didn't decorate tools or make mats or carved sticks. Her art ran the risk of looking at life in her own way. She moved without thought outside of tradition. She kept her work at home, only occasionally giving a small picture away, or tucking one in with a jug of goat cheese for someone sick or an old person who didn't get out.

Meggie died of a fever the same harsh spring that Donal decided to leave Millstone Nether. Madeleine painted a picture of the cemetery where she last saw her mother's pine box, and though it had been a drear day of thick fog and cold rain her picture was coloured in the bright yellows and greens of late spring. Along the side of the grave was a row of red tulips and over the unmarked mound of freshly turned earth a hardy crabapple tree showered pink blossoms over the earth. There were no mourners or minister, only a little woman wearing bright brocade boots sitting on a branch at the top of the tree. Madeleine called it *My Mother's Funeral* and tacked it up beside the picture she made of her brother playing double bass with two fishermen fiddlers at the wake in their kitchen after the pine box disappeared into the ground.

Donal persuaded Colin to travel with him across the sea. They worked as ship's hands and after many months, when they managed to get into land-locked places, they discovered they could make a living in the soot and filth and crowds of old cities by playing their instruments on rough cobblestone corners. Their jigs and airs and sea skin and great muscled arms made a sight and a sound in those places where men no longer used their bodies to make a living.

Resourceful and plucky, the two Millstone Nether boys traded on the novelty of their music and worked their way deeper into a Europe where court life and church life had forged a music too intricate for invention after hard days at sea. They took up with music students whose languages they didn't speak but who liked their dancey tunes and their quaint bowing. They traded music for music.

Colin spent fleeting nights in warehouses and small theatres where young musicians experimented with any sound they could record for dancers who moved their bodies in angular ways. He soaked in an idea of the world in which *bhavas* and blues and tonalities of twelve all came from the same source. He listened with an ear well stocked and weaned on rhythm and ballads. He collected hundreds of recordings, though he had little desire to master the playing of any of this music himself.

Donal began to train his fingers to the rigours and discipline of prelude and fugue. He thought he had found what he was looking for in strict counterpoint of the old music of Europe. He wanted a new bull fiddle and found a magnificent seventeenth-century Maggini bass. The aged virtuoso who owned it demurred that the bass was surely beyond the means and talents of such a young man. Human beings, he said, are granted only a single life. My instrument is stained with a length of experience beyond any mortal's.

He agreed to allow Donal to play it just once. He watched the young man caress the neck of the bass and he listened to him play Bottesini's "Allegretto Capriccio." He apprehended with sorrow that his exquisite time-shaded instrument had found a worthy new guardian. Donal felt the bloom of low sound vibrate through his body like a resuscitating breath. He heard in the Maggini's depths things that most ears do not discern. Its essence and beauty thrived in its unperceived lowest tones, like an elephant's inaudible rumblings. The night the old man finally gave it to him, he took it to play with Colin and some young students in a smoky bar below a restaurant. He played for them a piece he improvised called "Narcissus." At dawn a harried woman from the virtuoso's building rushed down to the cellar and told the students that the old man was dead by his own hand. The police were looking for Donal and the Maggini.

Colin said to Donal, Is it really yours?

He gave it to me.

Then let's go before someone decides he didn't.

The cathedral chimes did not ring another hour before the two young men were on their way to the nearest port, looking for a ship heading west. It was reason enough to go back. When they were out on the ocean walking the deck at night their home thoughts began to take up space. Donal said to Colin, Do you remember that girl at the greenhouse? Do you think she's married yet?

Colin answered, Can't know. Wonder if anyone got froze on the clumpers this winter.

They were embraced after their wandering by the extraordinary musicians of Millstone Nether, who took all they liked from the travellers and tossed off what they did not fancy. They liked Colin's recordings of music from mountains and bayou, isolated places like their own. He played them abbey and court music they admired but declined to play. They had little taste for his piano with bolts and erasers between the strings.

He's got high-learned, joked one.

He's jinking us, said another. That's not music.

So Colin picked up his fiddle and scratched out "Sandy

MacIntyre's Trip to Boston" as if he'd never left. The fishermen joined him with their fiddles and guitars and spoons.

Donal had been harder stirred up by his learning and left the kitchen party early, troubled by the restlessness of a young man confined. He went to see Dagmar at blind Norea's. They talked of the weather and the sea and planting, and he played for her what he could not speak. To his delight, Dagmar pulled out a fiddle and scratched along.

After her mother died, Madeleine Dob agreed to marry Everett, a poor fisherman thirteen years older than she was and so miserly that no woman on the island would take him. The only thing he liked to do was smoke.

He came by and said to Madeleine, Yer alone. If I moved in, would you like to keep house for me?

Madeleine said, I'll marry you if we spend equal parts on tobacco and paint.

There were some who said that Madeleine's was a bleak life with the mean little man who wouldn't haul in enough water, who hoarded the lamp oil and kept the fire so low there was frost on the insides of the windows all winter long.

If a poke-your-nose-in said anything about it, Madeleine answered, We get along.

On days when her hands were too stiff Everett did the milking. On days when he didn't feel like fishing he stayed home and smoked. The insides of the once-neat house became a dark shambles of dirty dishes and clothes piled up and the mixed odours of tobacco and paint. And those few who ever got inside the dank rooms also saw Madeleine's pictures of all the happiness of Millstone Nether tacked to every wall and stacked on sills and tables: the fishermen's big catches, Norea's milk wagon clopping through the settlement, the bright rush of a spring melt over the red cliffs, women holding children's hands, ice floes on sunlit days, the yellow and white and red dories turned upside down on the shore, cows nibbling the bushes, puffins nesting along the shore, cats under bushes.

Everett watched his tiny webbed wife tying her paintbrush between her fingers with old rags when her stiffness was too great and never interfered with what he called her dabbing. She watched him smoke with a certain affection for what is familiar and did not protest the cold or dark or smoke inside. They did not prevent each other from becoming more completely who they were, and because of this their marriage worked better than many. It was a comfortably taciturn thing, an arrangement based on not-mentioning. In that inhabited silence Madeleine was free to carry on her painting and her conversation with herself.

Norea taught Dagmar the jigs she knew from Ireland, hands hanging straight by the sides, all spirit in the nimble feet. But Dagmar didn't like to keep her hands down and she got the other girls to perform intricate clapping patterns as they danced in circles, one inside the other, spinning and weaving and clapping as if they were a single silkworm spinning its own shroud. They went out to the pole house and stamped and clapped and showed off to each other and when their bodies' rhythms floated down into the settlement the old people smiled. The boys' sport was to watch them through the bushes without getting a kick from one of those hard shoes flashing by or an insult from the sharp-tongued laughing girls who wore them. Able neither to dance nor to clap, Madeleine did not join in. But she watched and painted. She painted hundreds of pictures, preserving all their steps and all the patterns of their clapping for anyone who might ever take the time to look. And though all the dances happened after nightfall, she painted the girls in sweeping swirls of yellow light.

By the time Donal moved back in, Madeleine was making her new cheeses. She poured fourteen gallons of skim milk for each round and let it sour in the outhouse while Donal practised. He worked his way through his beloved Bottesini as she hoisted her large pot over the fire and warmed it up. She stirred in a little rennet to gather up the curds and Donal worked on Mozart's "Per questa bella mano." She hung her curds in a cloth and pressed out the whey. She listened to him as she shook fish salt through the soft curds, breaking them up very small. Then she carried her curds to a long wooden board beside the house. Donal put aside his bass and came out and watched her dump them into a round bottomless pot lined with a flour-bag cloth and set on a level stone. He saw her press the curds down evenly with her knuckles and gather the edges of the cloth up over the top.

The cheese is full of your music this year, she said as she placed a wooden top down over her mould, put two more heavy stones on it and sat down to rest.

It's warm, said Donal. It'll turn green.

He was in a mood. He was trying to shape and push his instrument, driven by something inside he did not understand. He heard what no one else did. His music made him mighty. His brow dark, Donal turned to Madeleine and said across the ripening cheese, I want to marry Dagmar Nolan.

Madeleine said, Have you talked to her?

Donal said, I haven't. I sit with her and her mother. I play for them. Her eyes are bright when she hears my music. I want to give her a dress. Will you make a dress for me?

Madeleine smiled. A wedding dress?

Yes.

But she's a high-spirited girl. She grows things better than anyone on the island. Some say she has powers.

I don't know about her powers, said Donal. I like her hair. She says she likes my playing. But I can't speak when she's in the room.

Then go for a walk with her along the shore.

Donal got up and walked the length of the cheese board. Will you make me a dress? he asked again. If she loves me she will hear my heart.

Madeleine shook her head. He was stubborn and cocksure. His music grew more inward and melancholy each day. He demanded service to his own talent and would not acknowledge another's. But she loved him and after her animals were settled she sat by the lamp each evening and stitched with her stiff hands. She made a strapless dress of black silk. It had a nipped-in waist and fell on the bias to the floor in soft folds with a hidden zipper up the side. After seven nights Madeleine finished it up, wrapped it in clean paper, folded it neatly into a box. She lined the bottom of the box with clean shelf paper. Then she tucked in a pair of antique dancing boots with small sculpted heels and long squared toes. Raised leaves of shiny gold and cranberry and royal blue swirled over the black brocade and eight round gold buttons arced down the outside shaft of each boot. They had travelled from across the sea packed in Meggie Dob's mother's trunk. They came with a long buttonhook, its ornate sterling silver handle boasting a tangle of tiny vines and roses. These things were from another time. Meggie Dob had sometimes danced in these playful boots, but Madeleine, with her rocker-bottom feet, was never able to put them on, though she loved their fanciful colours. She wrapped another piece of paper over the boots and tucked the buttonhook in beside them, closed the box and tied it with a bit of twine. Then she gave it to Donal, who took it and didn't even look inside.

Love is expressed better in fine words than in silent sincerity, she said to Donal.

He answered from his hood of bone, What would you know about love, living with buddy and the cows and a herd of goats?

Donal's bass did not ring perfectly with Dagmar's fiddle no matter how carefully he tuned. It bothered him. One evening after they played together he said to her, Did that sound right to your ear?

She laughed and said lightly, Whenever you play, it sounds right to me. You're a worrier and that's sure. She waited for him to put aside his instrument but he clutched it and fiddled with his tuning. The truth was she was in love with him, and though she played what he wanted her to play, though she stayed back from dancing with the girls in the woods at night to open her door to him, though she grew him vegetables from her garden to take home, he never could bring himself to say that he noticed.

He said, There are wood owls that repeat songs to each other exactly an octave apart.

He adjusted his pegs and she came up close and playfully stroked the wood of his double bass. She said, Let me tune your instrument, and touched her fingers to his on the tuning screw at the bottom of the strings.

Don't. I just got it right, said Donal. He smelled her thick earthy hair and he desired her. He wanted to touch his lips to hers but he clutched his bass and let his gaze fall.

She turned sharply then and said, It's late, Donal. I'm off to bed.

Donal carried his double bass outside and through the darkness back to the gloom of Madeleine's front room. Slowly he loosened all the pegs. The strings limp and silent he retuned, searching for the low C that bothered him most, and he dropped from the traditional tuning in fourths to a new tuning in fifths. With it he could play a clean octave below Dagmar's fiddle. He delicately twisted the tuning pins at the bottom of the strings, ran his fingers up their long length and adjusted the pegs again, turning and squeezing them into the wood of the neck. Then he struggled to find the old notes at new places on the fingerboard. For the first time in his life his low strings did not sound flat to him and his open strings were resonant and round as a fiddle's highest E. Tuned in his eccentric new way, the bass, he discovered, had the intonation he had always missed and he listened to his own playing with the awe of someone who has found a new species. He was excited by the sound and struggled to teach his fingers a new set of fingerings, which was as difficult as twisting the tongue around a new language.

The next morning first thing he took it to show Colin, who shook his head at his friend's exertions. We've always tuned the old way. Why change now?

Why set the dead as my measure? said Donal. I've got something here.

But it's the same music.

I make it sound better.

You hit sour notes because you can't remember where your fingers should be! said Colin. It's like shovelling smoke, no end to it.

Donal ignored him and wrote eccentric and appealing letters to the people at Thomastik Dominant strings. With the delight and excitement of a boy collecting, he received dozens of strings in the mail. He experimented and settled on an A and a G for his F-sharp string from the solo set, a D and a C string from the orchestra set. He wrote long letters pleading with the string makers to create a real G and a thinner C. He changed his bow hold and played harder into the strings, closer to the bridge, slower. He wrote to a bowmaker across the sea and asked for something different from pernambuco wood. Amused by the young letter writer's passion, the bent old bowmaker fashioned a new bow from snakewood, and sent it off and learned from a crumpled letter that the new bow tripped and moaned, strutted and sang.

Donal was shaping his instrument into the perfect prototype of the man he wished to become, full-bodied, nimble and witty, athletic and loving, commanding and tender. In his great and graceful old doghouse he now heard the rhythmic pulse of unexpected tendernesses, an inclination toward romance and a courage he did not yet know in himself. He became an ambitious creature both wandering and chained, striving to command the passion of his music and shackled to his lonely practice. Days and nights slid by when he spoke to no one and never left off his playing. The more exquisite his sound became, the more he believed that fate had decreed that all must give way to his music.

Moll lived in ebon shade, isolated from the people of Millstone Nether. She kept herself company with a little fish hook and a knife. Alone at night she laid strips of rags out on the floor of her hut. She crouched down flat-footed and leaned forward, so loose at her hips that her knees pointed straight to the sky to embrace her ears. She stripped naked to the waist and her long breasts hung forward limply. She caressed them with her cupped palms, stroking their sand-coloured nipples stiff and attentive between her strong thumbs and forefingers. She observed them through the empty slots of her eyes as if they were not her own. Then she let them drop, reached forward and hesitated briefly in her ritual decision between knife and fish hook.

In the first instant after the knife's cut there was no feeling at all, only a quick burst of blood beads along her expert lines. She was compelled by the fleeting dispassionate blade. The knife had traced a misshapen orb of white scars over her breasts, a history always incomplete, awaiting her next idea, a connecting thread here, a new cross vector there. Pitilessly she ground down all distinctions in her cuts. When she stretched her bony arms above her head or wrapped them around her back, she opened the wounds and could still feel an echo of night during the next day's light. Most see no meaning in the close recess of darkness but Moll knew otherwise.

The hook required both will and submission like two lovers, one who locks the door because certain violations are to be enacted and the other who feigns ignorance that the door is being locked. When her breasts shied from the searing ripping and the mind retreated, she forced herself, tearing against the barbs. She pushed and pulled the shaft, and tugged at torn flesh, and pricked the skin with the tiny point. And when she was pain sated she slid the hook out shaft first. This last clouded her eyes dark with faint and she dropped back from her heels and lay on the floor, waiting for her vision to return. Now she had done worse to herself than any other could do. Now she could once again withstand that which was without, that which refused to see what needs to appear.

She leaned forward over the knife and the hook and that night decided on both, the knife for her left breast and the hook for her right. She enacted her ritual agon, witnessed by her thought's dark clamour, and wrapped her bleeding breasts in bandages and crouched near the door, watching the moon's pale course. When her strength returned, she took herself down to the edge of the sea and removed her skirts and bandages and waded naked into the salty waters, hands stretched high above her head, bony fingers reaching to hold the ungraspable sky, her callused long toes gripping the sharp pebbles. She waded deeper and deeper until the salt bit her breasts and stirred in them renewed dying. Then she hung weightless, the endless waters washing at her blood. No deep could hold her immortal vigour. She purged her stinging body awake from its meditation in the cold of the sea. She crouched and caressed the new traces on her skin, her art and travesty. Her presence demanded to be known by someone. This is the life in the darkness. What cannot be seen must be acknowledged. What cannot be honoured must await trans-mutation by uncreated night.

When the spring was over with its sudden storms that drowned men who could read the shifting skies and men who could not, everyone pulled out instruments to play at bonfires behind Norea's house. Colin built up the fire and beat on a seed-shaped drum held squeezed between his thighs. Donal came with his retuned bass, his fingerings finally stamped on his mind and hands like a new mother tongue. Together Donal and Colin hammed it up for the winter-weary people as if they were busking on faraway cob-blestone. Colin licked two fingers and drew them firmly across the drum's skin, pulling an eerie moan out of the drum's hollow centre. As each wail faded he pattered his long fingers across the tight surface. Donal watched with an ironic cocked eyebrow, as if to say, Bogger on you, and pushed his childhood friend into more complex rhythms. The others in the settlement laughed at their boyish compe-tition and joined them with a choir of fiddles. Dagmar watched Donal upstage saucy Colin. Donal rested one arm on the purfling, a lit cigarette stuck between the strings and the top peg, and shrugged. He nuzzled his cheek against his old instrument as if he were listening through the wood and beat out a simple bass line. He let his bow fall to pluck out a pizzicato rhythm, using his thick thumb for the fat low thump that marked each shift. Projecting into the open air was difficult. He took up his bow again and worked with his whole arm and his strong back, bending and curving himself around his double bass. Up and down the forty-two-inch strings, Donal beat and caressed his instrument, his powerful fingers working deep vibratos from the strings. The flames shone on his forehead and he dropped his face in an attitude of penitence. Sweat beads fell on the dark varnish and deepened the tonality beyond the range of even the most appreciative ear in Millstone Nether. The crowd admired his playing, but when they wanted to dance, they called back Colin.

Colin set aside his drum, pulled his spoons out of his pocket, started up a textured patter and tried to catch the eye of pretty Dagmar from the greenhouse. He watched her examining his spoons flashing on his thighs and willed her gaze up to his face. Finally his eye caught hers and he grinned and winked only for her. Then he called lightly across the crowd, Lovely Dagmar of the green thumb, sing for us! Encouraged by her blush, he got up and pulled her to stand beside them. With her strong, sure voice she sang,

> The gardener's son being standing by,
> Three gifts he gave to me, me—

The pink, the rue, the violet blue,
And the red, red rosy tree,
The red, red rosy tree.

Donal played a light bass to keep her company and Colin left off his rattling spoons and sat near her feet. When she came to the last verse she raised her eyebrows at the crowd and made them laugh:

Come all you maids, where'er you be,
That flourish in your prime, prime.
Be wise, beware, keep free from care,
Let no man steal your thyme, thyme,
Let no man steal your thyme.

Norea heard a new and passionate colour in Dagmar's voice. But Colin grasped the young woman's hand and pulled her to sit beside him and after the fire burned down Dagmar followed Colin to the cliffs above the sea. Hand in hand, standing in the wind, Colin brought the young woman to him and kissed her and touched her breasts. But she heard a movement in the trees and she pulled away.

Listen, she said.

Moll stood in a hole in the shadow near a small grove of gnarled spruce, as if she were buried from the waist down. Her hands were wrapped around her front and clasped behind her. Her eyes were fixed on them.

Colin shouted, Go away, Moll. What do you want here?

Moll opened her mouth into a great gape, spat out some

fishbones, and said, Refrain from the kiss at a kiss-in-the-ring. Refrain forever or you're sure to be rinded.

Shut up your nonsense, Moll! said Colin, and he pulled Dagmar away and led her to the edge of the cliff. He sat and hung his legs over and said, Slide down with me.

Dagmar nodded, eager to leave Moll behind, and Colin gave her a good tug over the side. Together they slid down over the red earth, rolling faster until Colin took Dagmar in his arms and rolled log-style, shielding her with his own strong back and forearms. At the bottom they were covered with dirt and scraped and Colin pulled his shirt over his head and jumped into the sea. The sun was well down and in the darkness beckoned her to follow. In the cold water he held her again and whispered, She is all states and all princes I. He'd used this plenty of times with women when he travelled. Charm and love were all one to Colin Cane, a youthful confusion he enjoyed.

But his were the first such words to stir Dagmar's body, his the first fingers to brush her breasts, his the first tongue to touch her throat. She believed his words were spoken to her alone. She liked his light-heartedness and his loose-limbed body. She'd known him her whole life but he'd never until this night turned his eye on her. She made love with him and Colin pulled her up from the shore into the sea again to swim beside him. The cold saltwater washed her scent from his skin but not his seed from deep inside her. Puffins flew along the cliffs before heading out over the ocean. The new lovers swam back to shore, shivering and laughing and made love again, and Dagmar worried and Colin whispered, The first time is free, in the ecstatic moment before their son, Danny, was conceived. That night Dagmar's girl-life was over. Daring love's briefest flush, she'd been snared like a young rabbit on the straitened path.

Donal skipped stones with Colin and tried to persuade his friend to come away with him again.

He bent sideways and sent his stone across the water, chanting a boys' rhyme, a syllable for each bounce. A duck, a drake, a saltwater cake, he said. Colin, you can't do anything more here. You're going stale.

Colin grunted impatiently, skipped his own stone a clear dozen times across the surface and chanted, A duck, a drake, a saltwater cake and a bottle of brandy-o.

You didn't get to brandy-o, said Donal. It dropped! Don't you want to give your hand to more than the music here?

Colin skipped another stone and said, I want to sound like a musician from Millstone Nether. A duck, a drake. His coarse stone plunged after two skips.

You need to loosen the roots, cut down the branches, scoffed Donal, kicking at the pebbles. He sifted through them, tossed one away, looked for the perfect one, smooth and rounded.

I sound fine, said Colin. There are as many sounds here as there are players. He skipped another stone. There are people here who know more tunes than we do for all our fancy travels. I don't know half of them. And when I know a few more, I'll go to the mainland again.

Careful Donal found his perfect stone, skipped it so far out they couldn't see where it sank. That's a duck a drake twice at least, he said. Who'd want to hear our music there?

I like our old music, said Colin. I dream places to fish and I am always right. The only time I'm completely connected is when I play Millstone Nether tunes. I'm staying for a while.

Tradition is laziness, countered Donal. I've found a more perfect sound already.

They were heading along the shore to take Dagmar in the skiff up the coast and they abandoned the dispute they had repeated with variations through those shortening days. Being back made Colin light-hearted and happy to stay. Being back darkened Donal's brow and made him restless. He didn't have Colin's prodigious memory for the tunes. He was tired of playing at kitchen parties and tired of playing alone.

They found Dagmar already by the little boat, a sack at her feet. Colin took the centre seat and rowed cross-handed straight north up the coast past the rocky-man, each of them listening out of habit to waves roting the shore. They passed a bottle around. Colin pulled the boat into a little river's mouth far from the settlement. Dagmar was six weeks pregnant and she was irritated. Her body throbbed with the knowledge of her baby growing and the desire she felt from these two men who both wanted her. She was annoyed that Donal had given her no sign and that Colin was trying to take her over. She'd made no decision, yet a choice had been made. Colin was cocky. He kept her from her work in the greenhouse and sidled between her and anyone else who wanted to be around. He stirred things up in her and divided her from herself.

They settled down to watch the sea and they drank a lot. Colin said, Do you know what they do with a Chinese bride? They blindfold her and all the men come up to kiss her. He squatted, hands drumming his thighs restlessly, the sky rosy and thick with clouds. He said, Then they ask her which man is her husband.

Donal snorted drunkenly. The air chilled when Dagmar looked into the sky. Donal pushed Colin's shoulder roughly and said, What a thing! Colin shoved him back hard. Stripping off his T-shirt Colin said, Dagmar and I are getting married. Let's play kiss the bride.

Dagmar looked at Colin. What made him think she was going to marry him? What made him think he could say such a thing and not ask her?

No, said Donal.

Colin tied his shirt over Dagmar's eyes and said, Kiss her and whichever of us she chooses makes love with her here and now. The loser goes back to the dory and waits.

He took another drink and passed Dagmar the bottle.

He thinks he can just take over my life, she thought. She laughed recklessly and said, mocking them both, And what would make one man's kiss different from another's?

Donal shook his head and Colin said, Coward. Look, Dag's ready, aren't you? She's not afraid, she loves it. Don't you, Dag?

Dagmar had grown up under kitchen tables listening to women drink mugs of tea and talk of love as if it were a leaky skiff. Her father was nothing but her mother's memory. She could not reckon how her body still quickened at the sight of Colin in spite of her mind's strong resistance. Norea always said, Listen to your heart. But here she was nineteen and no man left on the island for her but these two wanderers. She needed to shift their attention back to her. She pulled off her blindfold and slipped out of her clothes.

I'm going for a swim. When I come back I'll be ready.

Colin and Donal watched her firm bottom disappear into the water. She wrapped the cold ocean like green lacquer around her and was pleased with the silence inspired by her nakedness. The young men shifted from their anger to wanting her, feelings twisted like seaweed around an anchor. She plunged into the light waves, freer than she'd felt in weeks. She returned shivering and water-beaded back up the shore. She patted herself dry with Colin's shirt and when he blindfolded her she had an idea.

Colin kissed her first, his sensual familiar kiss. His scent filled her and she softened all over again. His breath beat out a rhythm that filled her body and the sky. He wanted her but he couldn't own her, would never own her. He drew away and then she smelled Donal approach. His kiss was a fluttering tentative thing, an apology, a humiliation to be got over.

She pretended to deliberate and said unsteadily, as if more drunk than she really was, Colin is the second one who kissed me.

Silence slashed the shore in two. Colin cursed, picked up their bottle and drained it in a long drink, then smashed it on the rocks as he walked away.

Donal squatted beside Dagmar, untied her blindfold, picked up her shirt from the stones and awkwardly draped it over her. He said, You made a mistake.

Dagmar answered steadily, No I didn't.

His limbs were thin and eager as a boy's and his powerful fingers traced her body *da baccio* in the only way he knew to touch, but he could not speak.

When they drew apart Dagmar said, I'm pregnant.

He said, Already?

She laughed. Donal's heart went blank. He might have said he loved her, that he had always wanted to make his home in her, that he had a dress in a box ready for her, but he was perplexed by her cheeky heedlessness and could not think. He got up and dressed and handed her clothes over. Soberly they walked back to Colin and got in the boat together. The winds were blowing up offshore and the waves were high. The little boat tossed and slapped against the waves' funnels. Colin rowed them away from the land. Reckless, he pulled an oar from an oarlock and swung it over his head. Dagmar was afraid on the dark waters.

Stop your fabbing, Colin, she said. Let's go back.

I'm not going back. I like it out here.

Turn back, said Donal low and hard, the winds are up. We'll row double-handed.

Colin sat down unsteadily in the centre seat and turned them in a circle with one oar, the other laid across the boat, the winds tossing them out toward the open sea. Donal stood and moved toward the middle seat to grab the loose oar. He tried to push in beside Colin to put it back in the lock but Colin wouldn't budge. Donal reached out to shove him over, but as his hand grasped Colin's shoulder, the thick fist of his friend swung up and caught him on the jaw. Donal's head snapped back, then he lunged at Colin, who stood swinging the loose oar over his head. Donal grabbed at it and pulled one end down, trying to get in a punch but Colin locked his arms around Donal's neck, fell backwards and with two unsteady steps they were both overboard, still fighting in the water.

Dagmar could no longer see the shore. She grabbed the other oar and stretched it to them but a wave heaved her out of reach. She saw their heads washed over by cold waves. They'd drown. She stared hard at the sky and a strange rain storm whipped itself up over their boat spinning the winds around to drive them like tiny turtles back to the silent shore, Dagmar shaking in the skiff and the two men swimming hard to keep their heads above the water, beaten on by cold drops. Dagmar could stir up the winds and bring down the rains, but now she was overpowered by a man's love, a force she could not fathom. Each of them made it back to shore alone and half-frozen that night. In the marshland the fish and birds chattered.

Before dawn Colin tapped on Dagmar's window, beckoned her out and asked her properly to marry him. He said, I think I would die if the sea swallowed you. I almost lost you.

Together they walked up the shore to Madeleine's. Everett was smoking at the kitchen table and Madeleine came out of the goat shed.

He's gone, she said.

Where?

He didn't say. He came in soaked and said he was going to the mainland. Madeleine examined Colin's and Dagmar's faces and said, I wonder what you have done to him?

Nothing, muttered Colin. He'll be back. We always come back.

Madeleine shook her head with its little chin stuck on her neck and said sadly, Every way's likely.

Colin spent his summer's catch to get a thousand roses shipped in from the mainland to scatter all through his house for the wedding. Red and white and pink and yellow. From the front door to the bedroom he made a pretty trail and buried the bed in petals. Delighted, Dagmar stripped off her dress and dropped naked back into the roses as if she were falling into a pile of leaves. She read the banner Colin gilt-lettered by hand and hung over their bed: *Dagmar I am all Dagmar my head my heart my hand.* They lay heart to heart for twenty-eight days and Colin whispered to her, Dagmar, I love you, until the blooms were brown and drooping on their stems, until the petals on the bed were dry and turned to dust, until the water in the vases was spent. The people of the settlement loved a wedding and joked among themselves about the couple's lingering, Good thing there's a fall larder in there.

One morning Colin traced his hand over Dagmar's rounding stomach and, thinking about something else said, I'll tell you a story 'bout Johnny Magory. Shall I begin it? That's all that's in it!

Dagmar laughed but felt a fresh chill like ice-quar in the room. He was absent, his eyes trained on the door. He said, I want to go away to make my hand. A little one on the way and me stuck fishing forever.

Dagmar was ravenous and restive, her child soon ready for the world. She listened to his plan to travel to the mainland, to his dream to play his music, to record it.

He said in his charming way, Little sister, I'm a gatcher. I can't help it. I know if I go, I can get them to record Millstone Nether's music.

She looked through his man-hope and thought, Already his sweet love is sated. I am jealous of the bed he sits on, of the words he sings, of the strings his fingers play. Now he will leave and we will be two dead lovers, our bones embracing on the rocks.

The neighbour women shook their heads and the old fishermen watched with lips closed against unadmitted thoughts when Colin left and lonely Dagmar wandered up each day to visit her mother in the old farmhouse, to dig in the greenhouse, to keep making things grow.

Norea held her daughter's face in her hands, traced the dark disappointed rings under her eyes and said, There is only one first love. But secretly she mourned.

The light faded slowly from Dagmar's eyes. The young woman bore her beautiful son, carried him through her mother's greenhouse in a sling across her breasts, nursed and dreamed with him. Colin wrote fine letters from his wandering that buoyed Dagmar's girlish loneliness. She left them lying on the kitchen table and read them to her mother, proof that she was loved.

> My angel with all lullabies under your tongue, I'm coming. I hope your labour was not too hard. For my part I won't cry crack. I prick, peck, pluck and pull and they say they'll make me a record I swear it—for you and our son. So you see, my love, I have not escaped the labour either. I return on angels' wings in all haste.

Norea said, Romantic raving! Where's he when your sheets are cold? Where's your fish and brewis?

Dagmar said, Don't talk like that. He says he'll die without me.

Men have died from time to time and rainworms have eaten them but not for love, said Norea.

Dagmar folded her letters away. What would you know about it?

Love, said Norea, is the wisdom of fools and the folly of the wise.

There were portents and silences but Dagmar ignored them and slipped Colin's letters under her pillow:

> Dearest D,
> This room is too lonely for words, only a mittful

of people in the audience tonight. I have no rest from the picture of our Danny in your arms. He looks out of mirrors that before I saw myself in. He speaks to me in mouth music that words would only impoverish. He begs that I live at home with you and throw stones with him up the shore. But, dearest love, I am so close. Just a little more time. When we played kiss-in-the-ring under the sand cliffs by the breakers there was only one miracle could crown it.

Averse as he was to the first days and nights of mewling wide-eyed life, Colin did not return for months. He preferred his own disarray. When he did come back, a promise of a recording written in the flat language of the mainland tucked in his pocket, he held loving lonely Dagmar, her lips eager for his. The baby wailed in his crib in the corner of the green-house. Colin told Dagmar he had to go back again. To fulfil his promise.

And what of your promise to me? she said, throwing her trowel at him. What use to record a past that has no present in it?

The next morning Norea wasn't surprised to hear that Colin's clothes were lying on the ground, tossed out his door. Oh, oh, she said, now it begins in earnest. She tapped her way over to their little house and on the front step speared a pair of Colin's shorts with her cane.

Inside, the baby had a basket of eggs on the floor. He crawled with them to different hiding spots and broke them in a careful ritual. Dagmar was crying in a darkened corner of the kitchen when she heard the tap, tap of her mother's cane.

Norea pushed the door open and, feeling the coolness of the room, said, Why have you drawn the curtains when the day is fine?

Dagmar said, I tossed him out.

And his clothes too, said Norea, lifting her cane and twirling the shorts on it like ribbons on a maytree. She flicked them off onto the table and asked, What did he say?

Kill and bliss me, but first come kiss me, said Dagmar.

Even in her rage the young woman was charmed by his words and took pleasure in repeating them to her mother. She did not tell her that she had dragged her ring in a long cut down his cheek and left him bleeding.

And where would the wanderer be? asked Norea.

In his grave, for all I care.

He'll be back. This is his drowned father's house. He'll want his clothes, she added practically. Will you open the door to him?

Dagmar sobbed.

Colin sent home letters asking Dagmar to come to him, to find someone to look after the little boy. He wrote: Remember our single self a month in a bed of roses. Put your lammie on and pull back your hair. I'll be waiting for you with the first boat.

Dagmar crumpled up the letter and wrote back: And who's going to take care of the baby? Get rid of whatever dancer or singer it is this week and come back to us.

Norea opened her ear to her daughter's gaunt words and said, I left something like this a long time ago across the sea.

Don't start, Momma. I've heard it before.

I can't let you starve.

We're hardly starving.

He's the nevers.

Salt tears fell into Dagmar's weak tea. Look, she said, waving his last card above her head out of the way of the baby's sticky fist, He says he'll be back soon.

You opened the door, said Norea. A man should die off after the first romance like mine did. *Is mór an trua é.*

That's my father you're talking about, said Dagmar, smiling through her tears.

Norea sniffed. I loved him but you never knew him, she said. No need for sentiment. Colin's dazzled by his own concern and you're just another cut-tail. Bring the child back home. I'll give you the farm as it was given to me. You've a gift with growing things. I've never been able to grow things the way you do.

You won't be able to stand living with me, said Dagmar. I barely can.

I can't stand seeing you wasting away like this. Come, Dagmar. You have so much more than I did. Make your own decision.

Dagmar tore up all of Colin's letters except one, which she hid at the bottom of her trunk: Dagmar, my dear love, cry in dark hours. It's wicked to hurt each other like this simply from too much loving. Then she closed the door behind her and moved back to her mother's house.

And so it was that Dagmar and Colin never lived together
again. When Colin was home he came and tapped on Dagmar's window and she led him to the greenhouse where they
made love under a moon shining through glass. Over time
they thrived apart. Seasons became years and they achieved
satisfaction in their separate talents.

Colin became the unequalled source of the music of Millstone Nether. The people on the mainland were thrilled by
his tunes and his playing. They came to visit and Colin
toured them around to hear the old men and women play
songs others had forgotten and he spoke of his native music
as part of the great traditions of the world. His travels made
him renowned as a musician who kept to his roots. He was a
sponge that never filled and his knowledge was vast. Like the
ocean he absorbed all that entered, and when there was a dif-
ficulty he flowed around it.

For her part, Dagmar's fields and greenhouse were known
in the settlement for their dependable abundance. In the
early years after Colin left, she suffered much bitterness, and
storms tossed up many a ship and men died below the waves.
But time wore it away. Her strong mind was absorbed in the
cultivation of things that shouldn't rightly have grown in that
thin soil and for a long time there were fewer storms and no
more droughts on Millstone Nether.

Dagmar raised her son Danny like a plant, watering and
feeding and pruning, until one day the boy asked to live with
his father. The next two winters she brought on ice that
blocked the harbours and kept Colin at home with his son.

The people of Millstone Nether observed the little family

with their strange way of living in two houses and joked, They've knit their net with holes in it. And though it was not what Norea would have wished for her daughter, she only shook her head and said, Well, at least they're on the pig's back and I'm grateful for that much.

So it was that Dagmar Nolan and Colin Cane might have lived into old age, their love bewildering them until they died. But there's no certainty in human life that can't change from one moment to the next. Old patterns give way to new ones and something fierce begins unbidden. At the age of forty-five Dagmar Nolan got pregnant by Colin Cane once more and late one night in her greenhouse the birth pangs began. Dagmar resolved with hope that this child's life would be different. Time and trouble can tame a young woman but an old woman is undaunted by any earthly force.

PART TWO

THE
MAKING OF
DECISIONS

Only Dagmar Nolan could labour like that. She swayed away from the house along the rough path through the greenhouse door to the seedlings at the back. With each pain she bent double, buried her face in rows of bulbs, straightened, paced, rested, tasted her own grit and sweat.

Hard labour came fast to that wily aging body. She held on to a clay pot and squeezed until it burst and nicked her hands. Wiping the blood on her hips, she pushed her heels into the floor to find roots of their own. Blossoms opened and seed pods drooped all through the greenhouse as she dropped into her pain. The pores of the leaves breathed fast and deep, filling the damp air with heady oxygen. Dagmar groaned and sharpened her desire. Swallowing time she bent over, pushed like an earthquake and screamed a holy beatitude, Awwawwwa.

Above the dirty glass panes over her head night clouds scattered and temperatures rose as Dagmar groaned in her flesh, tugged out the shoulders, then slipped the body and legs of this newborn daughter in a skid of muck up along the length of her collapsed torso to her breasts. She looked with not a little awe into the grave wide-open eyes of a baby born taut and potent. She held the child close inside her wide green robe. Then she snipped the cord with a pair of greenhouse shears, pushed out the placenta easily, light and flat and slippery as a bit of water weed. Stray dogs ate the mess of blood and afterbirth, stained the floor with their wet tongues.

Dagmar wiped and wrapped her newborn daughter, listened to her breath, examined jubilant the colour in her cheeks and her tom-tiddler toes. She felt for her tiny heartbeat, counted her fingers. When it was clear that the child was whole and well, Dagmar sank back. She guided the baby's tiny lips to her thickened nipple and right away the newborn pulled down milk, the light of her eyes twisted into her mother's, two sets of stars fixed in the same constellation. The baby slept and dreamed her first dream in the world, of a pressing descent through darkness, of the taste of milk and the smell of air, of the feeling of weight. She heard in single chorus the sound of the sea, the rush of the wind and her mother's breath. As her eyes moved under their closed lids Dagmar swaddled her daughter firmly and with her free hand gingerly dabbed between her own swollen legs.

Outside, steps approached, tapping along the stones on the path, the door opened and Norea shuffled in on bedroom slippers. She croaked in her dry middle-of-the-night voice, Dagmar?

By the seeds, back here. I've got her. She came.

Woman-worthy! Norea cried out, scuffing toward the potting tables. How long have you been at this? Reaching out her hands to Dagmar's, she touched the baby's face, dropped her robe off her shoulders and wrapped up her daughter and her new granddaughter as best she could, then kneeled beside them, tracing the baby's body with her stiff hands.

Dagmar teased, She looks like you.

Norea wrinkled up with a pursed-lip smile. Two squashed heads. Don't be fooled, the black hen lays a white egg.

She wiped away a few tears but not before one fell and stained forever the top of the child's forehead at her hairline with a mark shaped like a little crown. Knots of blue veins stood out like pebbles on Norea's calves and the loose flesh from under her old woman's arms cradled her daughter and this new baby. She rubbed Dagmar's neck and stroked the child's head, the three of them coiled around and through each other like spring-wakening garter snakes.

Never perhaps ever have mother and daughter been closer than Dagmar was with the little girl she named Nyssa. Conjubilant. Roots of one below skin of other. Baby's eyes fixed on the light of *mater gloriosa* too soon to be *stabat mater*. Dagmar measured the length of her newborn daughter's foot with her index finger, wiped and dried and caressed that dimpling baby bottom and that oversized vulva. In the moment of birth she willingly became her daughter's cradle, her sleep's darkness, the comfort of her hunger and the first song in her ear.

She was Nyssa Nolan, daughter of Dagmar Nolan who unwittingly turned weather fair or bitter, who was daughter of Norea Nolan who stole her dead mother's boots and made life from tears, who was daughter of the first Dagmar who took her husband's name and died young after bearing eight children.

Luthiers say that the tautness of the strings ensures the potency of the instrument. If there were ever a child who leapt taut and potent from between her mother's thighs, it was Nyssa Nolan. From birth her feet never stopped beating the air. By three and a half she played everything she heard, her first pint-sized fiddle tucked under her chin, and her feet tapping across the floor. How she played has never been equalled before or since. Let the singer weave it into song, let it flow from ear to mouth, let it pass from old to young. Long-limbed Nyssa and her fiddle came and changed the music of Millstone Nether forever.

She never forgot a tune.

She had perfect pitch.

These two mysterious gifts alone gave Nyssa Nolan a whole and separate grasp on her world, a sureness of footing, a soaring of spirit, an inborn conviction that she commanded both heaven and earth. Only the realm of darkness was not hers from the beginning. Even as a child she never played anything exactly the way it was played to her. She put her little stamp on it with ornament and grace. She raised her arms straight up into the air, fiddle in one hand, bow in the other, a gesture at once of defiance and supplication. She understood that of all human expression music is most silent to meaning. She sought to wrest from it the line forward into full declamation.

They might have guessed that Nyssa was different if they'd known the lost art of reading the lines on a baby's feet, the curled-up toes and soft soles still more spirit-borne than earth-bound. The foot's long line in the middle speaks of voyages—broken, wandering, dangerous, lonely. The line below the hug of the big toe speaks of will, determination and the willing disposition of the heart. The lines from the little toes predict talents and capriciousness, the creases near the insides of the ankles, adventures in the world. The shape of the heel foretells fortitude and happiness, the curve of the instep, tragedy and sorrow. Good foot-readers used to watch a baby's kicking and predict long life or short, large spirit or small, read how the child would trudge or glide through life. Nyssa arced and danced when she nursed. Laid naked on the floor, she lifted her feet as if ready to fly toes first. She splashed her legs in the bath and thumped on Dagmar's thighs. In her cradle her feet kicked the air as if she were already dancing.

Dagmar marvelled at her baby's strength and was dismayed by her bloody-mindedness. On days when the exhausted infant would not let herself sleep, Dagmar lay beside her on the big bed, stroked the little crown on her forehead and lightly rested her own leg over the dancing feet. But the baby howled, blood rushing to her cheeks, her face drawn into a scowl of indignation until Dagmar gave way to her aerial dance.

Tap. Tap. Tap.

Dagmar was dozing with Nyssa on the bed when Colin tapped on her window with a small coin. She looked through the glass into his eyes, still impish at forty-five. His lips were drawn back in a slight smile and he beckoned her out with that charming tilt to his head. Dagmar tucked four pillows around sleeping Nyssa and followed Colin away from the house over the rough stones into the greenhouse. The plants were already swaying to the sound of his fiddle playing "A' Chuthag." When the last note of the song fell silent, Colin set down his father's fiddle and from behind a pile of pots picked up the mask of a stag adorned with real horns. In the silent flickering shadows he held up the mask to reveal one of Madeleine's bright paintings strung between the antlers. The picture showed a girl weaving a white cloth and a row of women and men gathered along the edges of a long table waiting to mill it. Colin hummed the air to an old milling song as he handed Dagmar the picture in the basket.

She touched the blood blister on his lip with her tongue and wanted him, but her breasts leaked milk and she pulled away. Colin followed her back up the path and into the bedroom where the infant stirred with subtle hunger. Together they admired her tiny limbs and face in the dark as Dagmar lay down to nurse, wincing at the baby's first strong latch and sighing with her milk's easing. Nyssa sucked well and strongly and Dagmar examined lazy Colin stretched out in front of her, his laugh wrinkles, the faded scar on his cheek where twenty-seven years before she had scraped her wedding ring hard down his face in rage. The baby dozed and Colin nuzzled into Dagmar too, sucking some of her milk for himself until she pushed him off.

Your hair's all clitty, he said, affectionately stroking her tousled head.

Yours would be too.

You'll be wanting me around more now, he said.

Don't get that in your head, you always caudle things up, she answered.

A girl needs a father.

I've been trying to figure a way around that.

His love was gouged into her like initials carved into a hardwood tree. In her eyes he still saw the young man he once was. Dagmar had been thinking about resting before she got pregnant. Colin spoiled all men forever for her. She'd fallen in love with him and was never able to shake him. Over and over when she was young she vowed not to see him but he'd show up at her window, grin, crack a joke, and it would begin all over again.

One night her mother stood on the balcony above them and dumped water on his head, but he only called up laughing, Norea, by what name are you baptizing us?

I'm not baptizing you anything, called the old woman from up above. I'm trying to drown you.

Warmed by Colin's inconstant flame, Dagmar fell asleep with her new baby and wished she could hold on forever to the peace she felt with this birth. When she opened her eyes a folded paper was tucked between her fingers and Colin was gone again. She read his familiar hand, felt her aching vulva quicken, scorned herself for letting him charm her. No matter what he did she couldn't help herself. Always and once again. And she read:

> Sing cuckoo now. Sing cuckoo.
> Sing cuckoo now. Sing cuckoo.
> Summer is a'coming.
> Sing loud cuckoo!
> Growing seed and blowing bawn,
> Sing to my new daughter.
> Through day's eve and dawn,
> Sing cuckoo now. Sing cuckoo.

With and against him all her life. Gods and mortals. Age and youth. The living and the dead. It all begins and ends forever and forever with a woman and a man, shadows of godlife, then comes passion. Dagmar stroked her new daughter's forehead with a mother's strong hope. This child would never suffer, not Nyssa.

Nyssa grew uncommonly tall with long legs and arms. From the beginning she climbed and fell. With her baby strength she pulled herself up from a chair to the table and Dagmar swooped in to catch her when she stepped over the edge. Soon Nyssa shimmied up trees to hang from branches and balanced on the railing of Norea's balcony. Her third spring she climbed into the apple blossoms, took off all her clothes and applauded herself. She would not fully inhabit her mother's farmhouse, preferring to roam the shore and cliffs. She never slept in her own cot in Dagmar's room. She wandered between her mother's big bed and Nana Norea's up in the outside loft above the kitchen, crawling in bed with one, disappearing in the middle of the night and awakening with the other. She liked to nestle beyond the back field near the sheep sorrel. She inherited her father's natural pleasingness and her mother's direct apprehension of the world. She enchanted everyone with her red curls, tart tongue, cocked eyebrow and buoyant step. Her mother and grandmother marvelled over her childish diaries, which they read secretly. The first thing she ever wrote was *I dremd nanas har smelld lik mulch.*

When the girl was still tiny, Norea pulled a little fiddle case out of an old bulb sack and opened it. She tightened the bow and rubbed rosin on the yellowing hair. Feeling with her gnarled fingers, she pushed in the pegs, turned one, plucked, listened, loosened, played again. She reached for Nyssa's small hands and arranged them on the frog and the neck.

She said, Child, here is a fiddle and bow. The ivory is chopped off screaming elephants, the strings are guts cut and pulled out of sheep still warm. The wood is hauled by slaves. This little fiddle is fashioned from the suffering of the world. Are you worthy of it?

Nyssa held on tight, put horsehair to sheepgut and played a single note. Then she picked out Norea's favourite, "The Nutbrown Maid." Music fell off the ends of her fingers. She fiddled and stepped with her brother and father at the summer bonfires in her mother's back field. She climbed into the apple tree and hid until everyone came out at night. After Colin put a torch to the beard moss, and Dagmar settled away from the smoke, and Danny beat his drums and played his whistles, and Norea took the flask from under her shawl and all the others from the settlement gathered with their spoons and fiddles, Nyssa leapt with a wild whoop from the tree to the very edge of the fire, dancing and playing as she fell through the air. Her fiddling could seduce a seed from the ground. They laughed and bade her keep playing. She could play all the traditional tunes and she liked to add little bits of extra bowing and drones. Everyone drank and rocked on old chairs until the legs loosened and cracked.

Danny drumming wild crashed first into the earth and Norea said in a loud whisper to Nyssa, Your mother uses those baffed-out chairs to keep everyone off balance. Nyssa ran to her brother and tried to pull him up from the ground, lost her balance and fell toward the fire. Dagmar jumped up and pulled them both away. The old folks called for more music from Nyssa. When she finally sat down in the first grey streaks of dawn, Colin took out his spoons and improvised rhymes about his spring-haired daughter:

Be wary of Nyssa
the boys will come kiss 'er

And right or wrong
I give her song!

I take it! said Nyssa.

She dances hey diddle
and takes up her fiddle
By her we're all smote
I give her notes!

I take it! said Nyssa.

Her fiddle's so cheeky
Not mild or meeky
Such a sweet singing voice
I give her choice.

I take it! laughed Nyssa.

The two old women in the house guarded the girl's world
with fierce affection, tucking her words under their pillows at
night, opening their own word hoards to her and telling what
they had learned from plain long years of living. When Dagmar urged Nyssa to get some sleep, the young girl spun
around to face her mother, one hand gripping the neck of
her fiddle, the other in a fist with her bow on her hip and
said, I like to be awake! The girl set her own ear, and fuss over
her as Dagmar did, Nyssa always slipped away. All that she
asked was that her will not be usurped.

The moon is no door. The future enters long before its orb is run. Nyssa wandered up to the woods, up to the gaze toward Moll.

There in a hole lined with blackberry earth squatted the bald-headed woman. She held balanced on one bony hand her bronze pot. With the other hand she ran a smoothed stick around the edge. The pot sent up a low echoing moan, mro ohoh. Moll stopped her hand's circling and the sound died out and she looked up. Her eyes lacked all expression and Nyssa could not tell if she would speak or not.

Moll asked, Are you compelled?

Nyssa said, No. I'm just here.

Missed the path?

Nyssa looked at the pot gravely and said, Can I try that?

Moll spat a dark spit. She handed up the pot and Nyssa held the pot out on the open palm of one hand. She picked up the stick and rubbed it hard on the side and nothing happened.

Slower, lighter, said Moll.

Again Nyssa made a circling motion with her hand around the outside of the pot and again she heard nothing. She looked up at Moll, her eyebrows raised.

Moll rolled a cigarette and reached into her dress for a wooden match. She scraped it against a rock and the flame appeared and she lit the cigarette and blew smoke through a black hole in her right upper incisor. Nyssa bowed her head and torso over the bowl and tried again. She felt the metal vibrate against her palm and through her wrist. She felt the sound and then heard it, hers a higher-pitched hum than Moll's low moan. She moved the stick on the rim of the pot around and around, playing with the sound, feeling the vibrations move up through her hand and arm and into her body. Slowly her ear was opening to the relationships shared between pitches. She began to move through her own darkness as if not tied with joint or limb or held in the air on the brittle strength of bones.

As she played Moll began to speak. Moll said that Nyssa's grandmother talked to her sometimes through the weeds and knew darkness but that most people turned from her. Moll said that she heard Nyssa play at the pole house and that she played well but there were sounds in her fiddle that she did not yet know about. She said that they are in the earth and she did not know if Nyssa was capable of hearing them but perhaps. She said some people are just born to it. Nyssa said, Born to what? Moll kept on. She said that some people are compelled toward questions and a kind of living that have no answers and some can tolerate this and some cannot. She said to Nyssa that if she thought she had come to Moll to play the pot that this was only an excuse but it was as good an excuse as any. She said that no one can say why one person finds darkness in her own soul and another does not. No one can say why. But if a person is compelled, then not to look means that the soul goes stale and stunted and she will languish and consume everything around her and will not know that it is her own spirit within that is being devoured. She said there were many things that stopped people from looking at her but that the greatest was fear. She said that when they saw, they lost their former selves forever. She said it was not safe to look at her or to be in her presence. She said there were others like her and she did not know their origins or where they might be and she had not met any of them but that they must exist. She said this was a world that kept turning from its own darkness and did not embrace it or sing to it or talk to it but tried over and over to forget it. She said Nyssa's grandmother Norea sang to her and she liked that. She said many things that the girl could not fully understand, but when she finally stopped, Nyssa laid down the stick and handed back the bowl and said, I am not afraid.

Moll answered, You will be.

The ashes of Moll's cigarette were long cold on the ground.

Hungry? she asked.

Nyssa nodded.

Moll pulled herself out of the hole and led Nyssa through the woods to a cache in the ground. She removed a pile of branches covering the hole and there were the remains of a newly skinned rabbit wrapped in leaves, head and tail hanging limp. She swept up some dry pine needles with her large hand and deftly placed some larger branches over them and lit a small fire. Nyssa watched Moll throw the carcass into a pan pulled from the cache and set it in the flame, reach her fingers into the fire and stand up bones from former meals that lay hidden in the ashes.

Nature likes to hide itself, said Moll. It goes much further.

Further than what? asked Nyssa.

Further than as if it knew its aims. Do you think it knows its aims?

I don't know.

It doesn't.

After cooking the rabbit for a long time she reached her hand into the pan and tore off the rabbit's back leg with a wrenching and a twist. Nyssa heard the femur pop and took the meat extended to her. When she bit into it, she saw that a maggot had crawled to the inside rim of the pan, slipped down and was getting cooked alongside the rabbit.

Why do you stay out here? asked Nyssa, wiping grease from her hand on the dirt.

Out where?

In the woods.

Moll pushed the rabbit to one side of the pan as if offering it again.

Nyssa shook her head. Moll picked up the rabbit and threw it into the woods. She put the pan back into the cache. Then she put out the flames with dirt.

Not all questions are wise, she said. Too much knowing makes you old.

I want to be old, said Nyssa.

Not yet.

Can I go inside your hut?

They sat in silence and Moll said, You come back here sometime.

In the winters the shores of Millstone Nether got iced in with great shifting ice floes. The young boys jumped from one ice pan to another, daring each other to float up the coast looking for seal holes, playing at being at sea. They leaped from one chunk of ice to another, laughing and wrestling, their backs cold against the ice on the open water. Briny air stung their cheeks and hidden currents taught their feet to submit to the whim of the sea. Nearly always someone fell in and had to race home to get dry, hair freezing, fingertips tingling. The other boys ran in a clump around the wet one and everyone scattered when the old woman or man at home caught the ice truant and scolded, I'll give you your tea in a mug! Only once in the living memory of the island had a boy slipped and got caught under an iceberg and drowned dead.

One snowy, bright dawn Nyssa jumped from Norea's bed and ran out into the cold and down through the settlement to her father's house. She pushed through the door into the front room where Danny slept and shook him awake. Let's go jump clumpers, she said.

Danny rolled away and pulled the quilt over his head, You're too young!

I'm not, you slowcome! She tugged at his covers and his arms, jumped on top of him and said, I'm going.

Too dangerous, said Danny and pushed her off him.

I'll go alone then, said the girl.

Danny hauled himself out of bed, dressed quickly and followed her down to the shore. Nyssa had already found a long stick and was testing it in the water full of small ice pans. She stretched her foot out to rock the thick ice, planted her pole and hopped on her long limbs loose in the cold.

Swiftly Danny jumped on his little sister's large pan humming with the swish of cracked ice. He squatted, and stared into the clear sky, letting strong-willed Nyssa test her arms and balance.

Don't go away from the shore, he said.

Why not? she answered, swinging her stick out of the water and spraying cold drops on his face.

Stop that!

Nyssa edged to the side of the ice, held her stick across the front of her and jumped to a pan about a foot away. Danny scrambled up and jumped after, calling, Springlegs, you'll have us both in the drink!

But the girl had stopped and was listening gravely to something up the cliffs.

Together they listened beyond the light clinking of the ice to the moan of cold settled over the earth and from far up on the gaze they made out the sound of Moll's pot, tiny variations in a pitch that slid along the tones between the notes.

Nyssa asked, Is it true men go to her at night?

What would you know about that?

She thrust her stick down her fingers, breaking the surface of the icy water and poled them farther out from shore.

I heard them talking behind Da's rooms, she said.

Danny said, Men should mind who's in the shadows. I wouldn't know about it.

He whooped, spread his legs and started to rock the ice. Hands outstretched toward the sky, her tousled hair aflame around her ruddy skin, Nyssa slid to the middle. Danny leapt to the next pan and the next, scrambling toward shore. Hard on his heels Nyssa jumped and slipped and rocked on the thick white rafts. Panting, she caught up with him as the off-shore winds stirred up. They were both stuck on a large floating pan and too far to jump to shore.

Now we're done, Danny teased, his quick eye searching for a way back. Stuck on the back of snake that won't be charmed!

The open water grew all around. Nyssa hurled herself toward the shore, slipped and fell. Her leap rocked the clumper and as she swam under the icy brine to the surface a thick blue and mottled iceberg blocked her passage. Down below the water, the clinking of the ice sounded like wooden bells and she did not struggle but was strangely drawn to these sounds she had never heard before. She hung below, still and listening.

Danny was standing waist-deep in the water now and he pushed at the heavy ice pan. He saw her limp fingers poking out, grabbed them, pulled her out sideways from under the iceberg and stood her up in the water. One arm around her waist he half lifted her up to the shore. Moll stood there at her full height, watching silent. Danny pulled Nyssa right past her, wrapped her in his own damp jacket and walked her back up to their mother's house.

I almost lost you under that bellycater, he said, pulling her
to him and soaked in saltwater, safe beside her brother, Nyssa
felt all the plain contentment of a girl much loved growing
up on Millstone Nether.

Nature abounds in what we call catastrophe.
All it takes is a little pressure. Storms. Floods. Mudslides. All
caused by pressure, the overturning of the old pattern into
something new. Time passes and old patterns are forgotten. But
they are not lost and can still exert pressure, remembered or
not. Consumed by either fire or fire. While Donal had tried to
prepare himself, Dagmar had walked away from him down the
shore, held his best friend in her embrace and he hadn't even
guessed that he was losing what he thought he most wanted.

The night Donal fled, Madeleine saw the freak hailstorm
over the ocean. She was bent over a pot of boiling haywater
for an orphaned goat. The warm scent of the hay clouded
up around her face and she filled an old baby's bottle with
the fragrant liquid, took the bleating kid in her lap and
urged it to suckle.

Donal pushed through the half door and shed his wet
clothes in a pile on the floor. He went into the back room and
returned with his bass in one hand and a travelling bag in the
other. He said, I'm going now. I won't be back.

You're leaving before light? said Madeleine, shifting the kid in her arms.

They're marrying. It's dawn soon anyway.

Half the island knew and the other half guessed, said Madeleine. Your friend's no friend, Donal, but it doesn't mean you have to go.

I'd choke every time I saw them.

He's a jader, Donal. Time heals.

With the bristling anger of a young man betrayed he answered, What odds is it to you?

Donal took his double bass and sailed out into the ocean. He had no heart for the great cathedrals to the west and so he found his way south into the scattered dream-rounded islands of the Pacific. He made his living playing in smoky bars where no one knew that his bass was three centuries old and few noticed it was tuned in fifths. He played a perfect intonation few could hear, and was absorbed in the inexplicable mystery of his sound. For three and half decades he picked up with small bands and played in exchange for a bed, a meal, his next passage out, settling with the unsettled on the Pacific Ocean. He played whatever was popular with Japanese and Indonesian and American expatriates, filled his lonely impermanence with their bar-room stories. He sailed on coconut ships and outriggers and supply boats, and protected his bass from Pacific salt and humidity and damp. He played against the rushing of tides and his highest notes drew whales up to the surface. He sleepwalked through the years and only his night dreams reminded him where he had come from and what he had hoped for. They tormented him with the incorporeal cries of lost seamen but each morning he shook away those dream hollies as if they had not revealed themselves.

He possessed nothing to keep him anywhere. One night Donal sailed with an itinerant birdwatcher who had a parrot that spoke fifty-three words of an extinct language acquired from its last living speaker. He was studying an island where everything was dying. Birds that had displayed themselves fearlessly had begun to dwindle in number and disappear. First to go was a flightless bird called a rail. The flycatcher, the bridled white-eye, the honeyeater became rare. Then the squawks and songs and coos of the kingfishers, crows and even the plentiful white-throated ground doves faded from the air. The birdwatcher puzzled over the disappearances.

Donal was wandering in the island forest late at night when he heard an unearthly cry and frantic wings beating above his head. He shone his light toward the roof of the trees and spotted a hapless crow stuck in the wide jaws of a common brown tree snake, genus *B. irregularis*. The bird's pinfeathers were disappearing into the snake's jaws, swallowed alive inside the muscled coil, slowly poisoned with each chomp and chew. Soon only the desperate beak of the bird poked out, squeaking like a baby. Donal stood and watched the snake slowly close its jaws over the tip of the beak, then drop its head in postprandial fatigue. The snake's eyes stared unconcerned into Donal's. He swept his light across the canopy of the forest and saw what had been there all the time. The night treetops were inhabited by a writhing mass of snakes in a constant agitation to eat. Thousands of them wound deliberately through the canopy, hunting birds and eggs. They had already eaten all the ground life—rats, skinks and geckos. Their slender muscular bodies stretched great distances between branches, and the birds who had no inkling of danger continued to build nests on the sturdy thick branches their omnivorous neighbours preferred. The snakes ate anything—*Hedmidactylus frenatus, Gehyra oceanica, Lepidodactylus lugubris, emoai slevine, emoia caeruleocauda* and *emoia atrocostate*. They ate the last Micronesian kingfisher on earth. They even ate the birdwatcher's pet parrot and those last fifty-three words.

Night after night Donal watched the snakes gracefully stripping off the life of the island, live winding sheets coiled round living bodies. They had no predator. They worked the roof of the forest like foreign cod-fishers, hardy, fearless and cryptic. They succeeded at the expense of others.

We cannot choose whom we are free to love.

Together Nyssa and Norea, wearing her yellow hat, waded along the shore, the young girl describing to her grandmother all she saw. Nyssa said, Nana! A huge spider nest hanging under the wharf, full of babies.

Reading the girl's tone Norea answered back, Let's kill them! There'll be hundreds of those nasty things.

She handed Nyssa one of her shoes and said, Get the mother first! The girl struck the big spider in the middle, watched it fall over and said, Nana! Its legs are waving.

Good, said the old woman. What are the babies doing?

They're all climbing up through the nest and out the top.

Take hold of the nest at the opening, said Norea, and sink it under the water!

Nyssa reached into the nest hanging from its strong sticky threads. She pushed her fingers under the cracks and she swiped the nest away from the wood. Norea stood in the water listening. Nyssa plunged the nest under the water and a cloud of baby spiders crawled through the opening at the top, swarming up her arms.

Nana! she cried. They're all over my arms!

Norea spread her wide old hands around Nyssa's thin arms and brushed them down, shaking them over the water, whisking the spiders from her own arms and hands and plunging them down under the water. Then she pulled the sticky web off Nyssa's fingers and put that under the water too.

Nana! screamed Nyssa. They're still on me.

Norea bent down and scooped great handfuls of sand up from the bottom. She slapped it on Nyssa's arms and a tiny shard of shell flew into Nyssa's eye. The girl brushed the sand and the last of the spiders off her arms then clapped her wet, salty hand over her face.

There's something in my eye, she said.

Norea walked behind her back to the shore and sat down beside her. She said, Take your eyelid and pull it down over your eye. Your tears will wash it out.

But the shard was lodged there and stuck. Nyssa said, I can't get it out. I need the eyestone.

Norea said, No you don't. Give it some time. Let your own tears do their work.

But the shell stayed lodged. Nyssa begged to go to Moll's hut and Norea, who never refused the girl anything, followed her through the back of the settlement to Moll's path of spat-out bones.

Norea called through the closed door between the skull of the whale and the spine of the seal, The girl's got something in her eye.

It'll go away.

Norea pushed the door open and Nyssa walked into the glooming toward the taste of earth. Moll was crouched down in the corner.

Moll said to Norea, Wait outside.

She looked into Nyssa's eye, then walked to the northwest corner of the hut and brushed away some earth and lifted out of a depression in the floor a little clay pot. She removed the lid of the pot and pulled out an oilskin pouch. She dabbed her filthy finger on her tongue, reached into the pouch and took the eyestone from its vial of sugar. While Nyssa watched, she rinsed it in weak vinegar water and three bubbles pushed out of the black spot in the middle and rose to the surface.

Moll said, Lie there, girl. She pointed her dirt-stained finger at a pile of rags in a darkened corner partly blocked by the stove. Nyssa lay down on the rags and she breathed in the sour odour of rancid rags and did not move.

Moll said, The girl's in the dark night. She lifted Nyssa's eyelid, dropped the eyestone into the far corner of the eye, pulled the lid out and held it down by its lashes on top of Nyssa's cheek. Moll said to the eyestone, Eat it up.

She took Nyssa's hands, pulled her long arms straight and laid them firmly by her sides. Nyssa dared neither open her eyes nor move. She listened to Moll walk across the room. For a long time she lay still, feeling a scratching along her eyeball. She let her good eye flutter open, followed by her injured one and saw Moll naked to the waist. She saw Moll putting a poultice on a sore festering red on her right breast. Both breasts were horribly webbed with cuts. Nyssa stared at the disfigured orbs. She shifted her head to the side to see more. Moll sensed the movement. She turned away, pulled her dress closed around her and turned on Nyssa who closed her eyes and lay rigid.

Girl, what did you see?

Nothing, said Nyssa.

What did you see?

Nothing, repeated Nyssa.

You saw something. Open your eyes. Sit up.

The girl sat up. Moll stood and moved across the room and squatted beside Nyssa with an unlit lamp. She reached under her skirt and handed Nyssa a long glass tube, then lit the lamp's tiny fire.

Put the tube over the flame, she said.

Nyssa lowered the tube over the flame, watched it stretch its blue centre, pushing through white and yellow. She heard it begin to sing a pure single tone inside the tube.

She felt the note against her eardrum diminish all other sound. Moll reached her great hand out and covered the top of the glass and extinguished not the flame but the tone. Nyssa sat back on her heels.

Moll stared through her blank black eyes and formed her lips into a grotesque circle over her decayed teeth and began to sing the same note the flame sang, hrhrhr. She slid on the pitch and settled and when she hit the note's centre suddenly the flame sang again with her, the same note, hrhrhr.

Moll reached across the flame, lifted the lid of Nyssa's hurt eye, and with her thumb and forefinger plucked out the eye-stone.

Moll said, Music comes from the shadows, and she looked into the injured eye. She said, Music is a kind of practice for death.

I don't know, said Nyssa.

Nyssa! called Norea through the door.

Wait! said Moll. The girl's still healing.

Nyssa listened to the flame. She could hear from far away the high-pitched cries of ocean birds and from deep below the earth the shifting and turning of mud-puppies. Nyssa asked, Can you hear all those sounds too?

Don't ask questions! She thrust a cup at Nyssa and said, Here's medicine.

The girl took a drink, coughed a little, and took another. She asked, What is it?

Hurt wine, said Moll.

Nyssa drank down all of it, the deep blue juice staining her chin.

Moll poked her and said, Out of the way! Awake! You're better and Nana's waiting.

Then she pulled her sweater over her head and said through the neck, Moll's in a pitty-hole. Leave her bide!

Nyssa slipped out the door, her head thick from the strong drink and she took Norea's hand. She led Norea home and the old woman told her to slip in the back way so Dagmar wouldn't see them. They went inside and up to Norea's loft.

Nyssa said, Nana, I don't feel so good. I'm going to the porch.

She took her queasy stomach out for air. Norea followed her, and when Nyssa felt her stomach heave, she leaned unsteadily across the railing and flipped over like a fledgling falling from the nest. Her tumble was broken by an apple tree, green fruit landing with soft thuds all around her limbs.

She lay looking up through the branches, unable to move and tasted blood in her mouth. Dagmar heard the strange thump and ran over to see her daughter lying on the ground, eyes groggy, lips stained blue. She asked, Did you just fall off the balcony?

Norea called down, Did she break her neck?

Dagmar shouted back, No thanks to you! She's been at Colin's by the stink of her!

Dagmar picked her up and carried her inside, laid her out on the kitchen table and went to work with flax poultices. In a cloud of raw bile and Moll's wine Nyssa winced at her mother's touch and threw up. Dagmar mopped her clean. She needed to keep her awake and bring those eyes round from the back of her head.

Nyssa, she whispered urgent and firm, Nyssa, wake up.
What?

Dagmar helped her off the table and led her into the big
bed and sat beside her. The girl's eyes rolled back into her
head and Dagmar was afraid.

Stay awake, she said. Open your eyes, Nyssa. Look at these
seeds.

Nyssa whispered with a weak, cheeky tilt to her chin, Did I
just fall off the balcony?

Looks like it, Dagmar said and lifted Nyssa's head. It rolled
off her mother's open palm and her eyes sank back.

Wake up, Nyssa! said Dagmar.

The girl struggled to open her eyes, struggled to please her
mother. She said, Tell me the flax story.

Dagmar raised her head on a pillow and said, The flax is
buried and rippled, retted and spun. You hide it in the dark
earth. Nyssa, wake up.

She had to keep the girl awake. She said, The blue flower
opens to the midday heat and the lashing of rain. Then
people pull it out root and all. They drown it, roast it, beat it,
heckle and comb it. Nyssa! Open your eyes. You've got to stay
awake! What did I just say?

The girl asked groggily, Then what do they do with it?

They spin it to thread, weave it into linen, cut it, sew it into
shirts worn till they're rags. Do you hear me, Nyssa? Can you
talk? How old are you?

The girl opened her eyes again and tried to talk. I'm thirteen, she said.

Nyssa, what day is it?

The day after the night before, she said and struggled to sit up.

Seeing her eyes back firmly forward, Dagmar said annoyed, That father of yours won't start you drinking already! I'm fed up with Colin leaving me the clobber to pick up. I won't have you flying off balconies.

Red hair tangled around her face, a seed fallen to the earth and dying to sprout again. Nyssa grinned her father's infuriating smile. Dagmar brought her eight drops of spruce tea in a cube of sugar. Norea came into the room with soup. The two women perched like birds on the side of her bed.

Nyssa said, I feel awful.

You'll survive, grumbled Dagmar. Try to sleep. Morning is wiser than evening. She couldn't think what she'd do if the girl broke her skull and disappeared out the cracks forever.

Nyssa turned to her grandmother and said, Nana, I swear before you I will never do that again.

Don't you worry, smiled Norea, half the lies we tell aren't true. Your hair's like a birch broom in the fits, she said, running her hands over the girl's head. Be capable of your own distress. Do what is required.

Nyssa said, Nana, how does the eyestone work?

Has she been with Moll? accused Dagmar.

Norea and Nyssa fell silent.

Mother! cried Dagmar.

She'll leave her alone, said Norea.

Nyssa said, I don't want her to.

Dagmar asked, What would you mean by that?

The girl said falsely, I don't know.

I don't want you there again, said Dagmar. She already blinded one of us.

Did she, Nana? asked Nyssa. How?

There are two kinds of wisdom in the world. Judgement wisdom abides no blurred lines and no softening circumstance. Nature wisdom has black in its white and shifts with the day, the feeling and the temperament. Some say it is best to practise judgement wisdom on oneself and nature wisdom on others.

Nyssa had witnessed in Moll's hut what no one else knew, but she laid her hand on her mouth and neither judged nor spoke of it. And though her mother told her not to, all through the years when she was growing from a child into her own fierceness, she kept visiting Moll's hole lined with blackberry earth up on the gaze. Sometimes Moll talked and sometimes she showed Nyssa the bones she found in the woods. Sometimes she played her pot and sometimes she threw stones. Sometimes she stared silently from the naked orb of her head, eyes blank, a source of little visible delight. Nyssa could not say why she went to the bony woman, only that she was drawn to her, as if Moll were some part of herself. Moll belonged not to the island but to its caves and holes, to a place that is dead to the world above. Hers were raw and devouring passions, and loveless. And yet, when Nyssa lay on the ground beside Moll and put her ear against the pine needles and listened to the thick echoes from the rocks beneath, she sensed with the uncanny instinct of a daughter of Dagmar that birth and death are of a single essence and that she knew little of either. These were things she did not have the words to say. In the low moaning of Moll's pot she heard music beyond what she could play on her fiddle. Most people are, once or twice in a life, drawn to things that may harm them and that they cannot understand. Things that are necessary.

She came home from her visits to Moll and stared without seeing, listening to all the sounds of the island until Dagmar chided her. But Nyssa was absent in the way that silence is absence from sound. She played drones in her fiddle tunes until the people complained that she ruined the danciness of the music. They said that no one had ever played in this way before and that it didn't sound right.

Nyssa said, It's what I hear.

She was not afraid and she played what she wanted. Fierce and dancing, she followed what she was drawn to. Her ear was open.

One night, after they'd finished their snaking, Donal played an old tune while the birdwatcher laid out the bones of a bird, trying to figure out how the skeleton went together. What's it called? he said.

Donal thought a moment and thought again. I can't remember.

The other man shrugged, turned the little bones of the ribs around and said, It doesn't really matter. They all sound alike.

But they didn't and Donal couldn't remember. He leaned his bass against the wall and seeing the pattern of the bird's ribs quickly rearranged them in order, only the second one missing. Something in his ear was dying and he with it.

Why do you stay so long out here? Donal asked.

To see the end of the world. The birdwatcher admired Donal's quick eye. He could catch a snake, drop it into a bag and tie it shut with his teeth before the snake flung itself up and attacked. He could look at scattered bones and see the living creature's shape.

Is this place the end?

Could be here. Could be anywhere.

Is that the only reason you stay?

There was a woman but she left. She said she couldn't breathe when I was there.

Donal worked on the fine bones of a foot and shifted the small skull out of the way. He said, We say that we stay for love, run away for love, but a woman just goes firmly on in the same place being herself.

You?

I did not tell her that I loved her. She went with my friend. I didn't try to change her course. This is the truest love.

Where will you go next?

Donal hesitated. Don't know, he said.

What was to follow? Donal's hands were scarred with snakebite. He fished and climbed coconut trees for milk, wove fronds to replace worn thatch. But the hot winds never felt right against his skin.The sea is subtle—dread creatures glide under it, treacherously hidden beneath the loveliest tints of azure. An island, Melville said, is like a place in the soul, full of peace and joy, encompassed by all the horrors of the half-known life. Donal stared at the bones of the birds devoured by snakes and said, There's an island up north where an old woman used to bury all the birds that broke their necks on her windows. That's where I'm going next.

He wanted to hear the old men at night. It was time to go back. Before everything disappeared. Colin would know the name of that tune.

Nyssa put on Norea's old honeymoon negligee and danced a one, two, three around the old woman.

I've got on your lacy nightdress, Nana, she said. I like it.

A nightdress like that is not meant for keeping on as much as for being taken off, said the old woman.

Nyssa admired her own round breasts under the thin material and looked across at her grandmother's sagging skin. She said without thinking, Will I turn like you?

A woman must be as her nature is, said time-shrunken Norea to the heedless girl.

Nyssa wandered out and up to the gaze in the nightdress. She smelled the smoke from Moll's short pipe.

Girl, called Moll, a woman only is free to be very hungry, very lonely.

She held out the pipe to Nyssa and said, Have some dudeen.

Nyssa took the pipe and drew and swirled the smoke inside her mouth. She watched Moll stick a piece of grass through a black hole in her tooth and pull it out the other side. When the pipe went cold, she handed it back, and with her long bony fingers the woman stuffed it with more crumbled leaves, held a match to it, sucked and said, Can't stand a ring on a man's little finger!

Nyssa! called Dagmar from down the shore.

The girl squatted lower in the hole and said, I'm not going.

She was weary of the calling from home, drawn to Moll's hole as a wanderer is to the morning ship.

Nyssa! called Dagmar.

Weather's misky, said Moll. A man with a ring on his little finger thinks he's the jinks. Seen one on a fishing man? On a sailor? Mainlanders have 'em.

Moll reached between her legs, pulled out a small ring, and handed it over to Nyssa, who held it up in front of her, and asked, Is this a pinkie ring?

Moll nodded and with a whoop Nyssa stood up in the hole and threw it as hard as she could over the edge of the gaze.

Moll's cracked lips twitched and she waved her naked hands in front of her face. All gone, all over, girl. I'm hungry.

Nyssa handed her some biscuits from the nightgown's pocket. Moll stuffed the whole package into her mouth, spitting out the paper as she chewed, crumbs spraying down her chin. A fine rain began to fall.

Moll pulled a tattered rabbit pelt from under her heap of rags. She draped it over Nyssa's head against the rain, pulled off her own thick and filthy sweater and buttoned it around Nyssa.

In the drizzle Moll held up her hands to Nyssa as if they were a mirror and said, Where's the girl?

There is no more girl, said Nyssa. Only a hare.

She made the sound of a hare by closing her lips and squeezing air between her tongue and her palate. I will write down this song and play it on my fiddle.

Writing makes the spirit lazy, girl, said Moll, tapping her long fingers on her hairless head. A fixed word risks becoming a dead word. Hold it in your ear.

Nyssa did not understand. She scrambled away and headed down to the shore and Moll called after her, The girl is as the girl does.

By the time she was eighteen Nyssa had absorbed all the music Colin had to give her. He wanted something new for her birthday and chose Bach's "Chaconne in D." He handed it to her and said, A chaconne makes much out of little.

Picking up her fiddle and nimbly playing at sight, adding her signature drone, she said, But, Daddy, I want to dance!

Colin laughed. Bach is the essence of all that can be made in music. Will you get rid of that drone. It's making us all mad.

She shrugged. I like it. I want it to be like the sea always there. To speak of the sea is to refuse to speak of yourself.

Colin shrugged. Can't tell you anything. Like your mother. Here, I have something maybe you will like.

He went to his junk drawer in the kitchen, pulled out some old screws, a couple of erasers, some nails and a bottle cap. He dropped them into Nyssa's cupped, waiting hands, led her back to the old piano and lifted the front off. She smelled the musty insides of dry wood and metal, saw for the first time the guts of the whale. Eighty-eight felt-covered hammers were lined up imperfectly, waiting to be plunked against the rows of strings. Inscribed on the coppery pin-block were pictures of nine prizes and the words of a crafts-man's pride: *Above Medals of Merit Awarded to Us at Exhibitions Throughout the World.* It was piano number 19407 stamped in black on the upper-left-hand side and inscribed along the curve of the back was *Heintzman & Co. Toronto, Canada. Agraffe Bridge Patented March 10 1896.* From the vantage of Nyssa's four-stringed violin, the row of musty hidden strings was exotic. Colin lifted out the piano's action and turned it over. The very first tuner had scratched his name into the wood: *Bob 1900.* Nyssa ran her fingers over the dead man's mark and her father watched.

It's nothing but a big drum, he said, putting it back together. Here, hand me a screw.

She watched him choose objects from her hands and squeeze them between the clean row of strings until it looked like a rag mat.

Play, he said.

She sat down and looked at the piano's insides. She placed her fingers on the ivory keys. She played a simple C major triad. There was a clank and a thud, a note and a cluck. She sped it up, changed keys and syncopated the rhythm to hear the drumming clanks of screws and thuds of rubbers.

We have to get this down! she said in delighted adoring, as if she were the first to hear it in the world.

Why? said Colin, What are you going to do with it?

Make a new tune! said his exuberant daughter. She shook loose her kinked hair, put her hands on the keyboard and played another rhythm.

Colin listened and poured himself a drink. Danny wandered in to listen too, pulled a rack comb and tissue paper from his pocket and played along with his sister.

Nyssa insisted on writing down her father's music. They laid out long sheets, labelled the strings and noted where each eraser, screw and nail had been placed. Colin smelled the fresh salty scent of his daughter's skin as they sat shoulder to shoulder. Nyssa imagined their writing to be an affair of posterity, caught in the fleeting moment.

She came home to Dagmar that night alight with the pleasures of writing something she thought completely new.

Her mother saw the glow of a girl in love and asked, How was your birthday?

Fine.

Did he give you a present?

Bach, said her daughter dismissively. But he's showing me how to write down a song for a piano all stuffed up with nails and screws.

Dagmar too had once been Colin's private audience on that old piano. She had watched Nyssa thrive under his teaching, heard the girl's fiddling grow stronger and wilder. He'd taught her everything he knew, played tapes of the old people and recordings from abroad. His musical range was now hers and she excelled effortlessly beyond any other musician on Millstone Nether. Everyone could hear Colin's stamp on Nyssa's playing, her easy shifting between styles, already a master of the tradition. Dagmar thought, He is a bridge to her own spirit. Heaven only knows if the bridge will hold when she plays all that's inside her. He never could bear anyone else's ferocity.

Years are drops wrung from a rag. Still tethered to childhood, Nyssa was ready to leap, knowing little of flying. Music was her haunt. She played what she liked. In ancient times and distant places the people would have honoured her, a young woman alive to her own song. They would have beat drums and danced for her. They would have brought young men to her door and they would have sung, Like her lips, sweet is her vulva, sweet is her drink. But that song was lost long ago and Nyssa would have to find her own way. She was destined. To go, deeper, darker.

One Saturday night Nyssa gathered four boys with their fiddles and guitars and made them arrange themselves like a thick tree trunk in front of her. She led them to the pole house stage and when everyone arrived for a time, she hid behind them while they sang a sweet air together, then out she jumped from behind, the boys spreading like branches to both sides of her. Nyssa, centre stage, was the root to which all eyes turned. She put bow to strings, her flesh all power and excitement, a young girl standing exposed as a blade of winter grass in front of the flickering lanterns. She whooped and pounced on the first piercing note of "Nana's Boots," a medley she'd made up herself. The old people shook their heads at her showing off and called her a regular philandy and laughed. She knew how to pump it out. She danced and fiddled, wore her longing and hope naked for all to see.

She had a knack for the stage. She made nothing so appealing as her own fearless energy. She called at the crowd with a cheeky swing in her tight black jeans and when they called back to stop her showing off, she sidled up slow and unpredictable to the edge of the stage, paused, leaned in and whispered, suddenly girlish and sweet, Oh no, not yet. Everyone laughed and someone called out to do her medley again and she feigned breathlessness and said, I can't do that one twice, then winked before hitting its first note once more, anointing them with all they desired. She played the Millstone Nether people as well as she played her fiddle and they loved her. She sensed their moods through her skin and mirrored everything back. She filled their ears with lovers' ballads. She played each person's secret cravings. She stamped and spun across the stage, seducing, daring them to join her. Her face was the shape of a flax seed, nose straight as a clean punch, body nipped in at her waist, eyebrows set in a quizzical arch. She lived in the upper and lower registers.

Dagmar stood at the back of the crowd, listening.

Her daughter was alive with something a mother couldn't prune. There wasn't a boy on the island who knew which key she'd play in next. She played at all the weddings and parties and had plenty of tunes left over. There wasn't enough space for her to fill. Those last nights before she disappeared, she played out in the woods, down the road from her father's house. Under stars and moon, lips red, hair red, skin wrapped in black, disappearing into shadows as she step-danced, broken horsehair flying loose and catching the light like fireflies, her sheepgut sang a young woman's reckless wonder at the world. Her toughened fingers pressed and slid, tapped and plucked, her green eyes fixed on things beyond, and still faster she stepped until she disappeared into notes in the night. Nyssa of Millstone Nether.

Donal appeared in front of Colin's old house, a set of bass notes playing in his head.

He smoked a cigarette in front of the half door and didn't ring the bell. He loitered, tempted to turn and leave. Then the door opened and there was Colin, unshaven and just waking up.

Haven't had tea yet, come in! he said without looking as he rubbed his hands through his hair.

Donal silently pulled out another cigarette, stuck it between his lips and lit it with one hand the way the two boys used to practise together. Colin looked through the smoke to finally see who was there. The eyes do not change when everything else is altered.

Donal?

He stepped back, took the cigarette out of his mouth and cupped it by his side.

Colin pulled the door open to embrace his old friend and Donal stepped backwards to avoid the threatening arms. Few had touched him all those years. Colin dropped his arms and stepped back too. Unabashed, he said, Got a smoke?

Donal tossed him a cigarette and damp Pacific matches.

Colin tried to light it with one hand but he was out of practice. Soothing, sharpening nicotine seeped through. Where did you go? he said.

Nowhere. Away.

Donal examined the feeling of being recognized. He watched Colin step back inside and wave him in.

Where's Dagmar?

She doesn't live here. We split up. A long time ago, a few years after you left.

You left?

She left.

Still on the island?

We raised our children together, more or less.

Children?

Two. A son and a daughter much younger.

Colin stared curiously at the scars on Donal's hands. Donal followed him into the kitchen and nodded when he held up the whisky bottle.

What did you do?

Collect dead birds.

Colin handed him a glass.

Still play?

Donal didn't answer.

Seen Madeleine?

Yes.

Why dead birds? asked Colin.

Snakes.

Snake-eating birds?

Bird-eating snakes. Anything-eating snakes. It's all dying out there. They talk about half-lives. It is a place full of snakes. Back-fanged. He held out his hands.

Colin nodded. Here for a while?

Maybe. I built a place across the strait. Donal hummed out loud the tune that was in his head. What's that called?

"Ships Are Sailing," said Colin absently.

The name came back soft and sure as a fog-bird on the wing. Donal thought, Now I can leave again.

Bung your eye! said Colin lifting his glass. Feels like I'm waking from a dwall seeing you here. I'm going to Dagmar's tonight for a bonfire. My little girl, Nyssa, fiddles like the wind. You should hear her. She can fiddle anyone into the ground. Still play?

Donal nodded.

Colin stood, his fingers loose on his glass, and studied the familiar stranger. Then he reached across the space between them into Donal's shirt pocket and helped himself to a cigarette.

Nyssa dreamed smells. She dreamed she was wandering in a place lit by fireflies. The dusk gardens were scented with purpurea and sweet peas, overrun by unruly pink performance her mother had planted. Sweet alyssum warmed the air. The day had been suddenly hot and then just as suddenly it had rained and the perfume from damp cedar and sweet grass filled the night air. Partyish bursts of laughter came from bowers in the trees and a voice said, She's coming into ear. From behind the gardens in the dark shadows Nyssa saw Moll in a cage. She said to the cage dream-rudely, What are you doing here?

Moll spat sea moss from the side of her mouth and said, Who do you think made all this?

Then Nyssa woke up.

Nothing could wait. Appetites and desires had to be satisfied.

All day and into the evening, Colin and Donal smoked and drank, saying little, their mouths growing cottony, their minds liquor clear. Colin went to the half room out back and brought in an old double bass. He leaned it against his piano, eyebrows raised in invitation. He sat and tinkled a few notes on the chipped keys. Donal allowed himself to smile, butted his cigarette, tightened the old bow and tenderly tuned the worthless instrument. The moment the bow hit the strings, Colin knew that Donal had never stopped playing and he listened with surprised affection to his old friend. They had little to say to each other, but they played, picked up old melodies and rhythms. Each listened and judged the other. Colin admired Donal's perfect ease, and Donal still judged Colin lacking. When they finished, Colin passed the bottle to Donal, who tipped it up over his lips and stroked the old bull fiddle affectionately.

Did you record? Donal asked.

Did, answered Colin. Lots of the others on the island too. I played over on the mainland for a while. Toughest audience is still here. Then he stood and said, Sun's down.

It was a slight spring that year, undependable. Dagmar had planted a clump of love-in-a-mist beside Colin's door. Starry rose and white flowers hung luminous in the darkness on a gentle tangle of pale ferny leaves. Colin snapped off a twig and twirled it in front of his face. Something thick in the air.

He stared at a great flock of shearwaters flying in from the sea, circling and diving and settling in the waters of the harbour.

He nodded toward them. Look at those bawks so thick on the water you could walk on them, he said drunkenly.

No snakes, said Donal. This was what it was to be the prodigal home, feasting and smoking.

Time to go, said Colin. Smart few'll be there tonight.

Donal stretched and said, Not going.

Of course we're going. I always go.

We're?

She'll want to see you.

Not going.

Colin stared hard. Then he thought of something. He went back to his room and came out with a pair of old oil pants, scissors and two tattered quilts. He cut off each leg and cut out in each a pair of eyes and a mouth. He pulled one over his own head and a hat over that and handed the other leg to Donal. He wrapped a quilt around his shoulders and gave the other to his friend. They'll never know you in this old cadder, he said.

Donal slipped the hood over his head. Only his scarred hands showed. They stood face to face in their disguises, eyes shining through the rough holes, delivered from the bond of identity. Years Donal had lived lean and monkish, the only other voice his bass. Pulling down his hood, he said, She'll know my voice.

Don't speak, then, said Colin. Hide your face as long as you like.

Nyssa was starved for her own ferocity. Born to it. Her ear was set. The music was written; nothing to do but play.

The flames of the fire leapt high when the two shrouded figures wove across the field toward Norea, Dagmar and Danny, neighbours and children waving flaming sticks and leaning too close to the flames.

Nyssa saw them first and shouted, Daddy! and ran across the field to welcome the gowned men. Why are you dressed up?

Found me out already! said Colin. Don't tell a soul. We have a friend who wishes to be hidden. I'm keeping him company!

Dagmar was irritated with Colin's games and strangers. And Danny had that day informed her that he was the father of Marta Morris's about-to-be-born baby. She sat beside the girl, who was uncomfortable and huge. Colin and his stranger were thirsty, and Danny poured them jars of whisky to sip through their hoods.

Nyssa disappeared into the apple tree and with a whoop jumped down, danced and fiddled toward the fire. Everyone laughed at her familiar trick. One of the boys took Colin's drum and joined her, making the skins moan and throb as he'd learned from the older man. Nyssa danced over to drunken Colin, who was already beating his spoons, and she tipped her fiddle down to play into his mask. The men laughed to see the two of them, and applauded the children following Nyssa's wild dance.

Dagmar, I'm not feeling so well, said Marta.

Here, lean back on me a little. Look at Nyssa. She'll be exhausted again tomorrow. Danny! Come over here. Are you going to make him take care of this child?

Norea called to Nyssa, Play my duck song.

The girl lifted her fiddle and the old woman rose and found some square footing. Her clear, thin voice chiselled at the night air through Nyssa's strings and her song made the children shiver.

> My momma cut me and put me in the pot;
> My dada said I was purty and fat;
> My three little sisters they picked my small bones,
> And buried them under the marble stones.

Norea had been blind so long that she'd forgotten the shapes of things. At first she had dreamed in images and colours. But they faded and disappeared and now her darkness was filled with the sensations in which she lived. She could hear the sea on the shore and smell the pine and the sweat of her family. She could smell the thick spruce beer Colin was drinking, that charming mocking manlife that Dagmar took for herself. Now there was a great-grandchild about to be born. What happened to all my brothers? she thought as she sang. Some most likely dead now. I never saw them again.

When she finished and sat down and the scattered clapping stopped, the stranger planted his double bass into the earth a little removed from the fire, flames flickering off chipped varnish. Nyssa listened to his first notes, then lifted her fiddle again. She stepped up his melancholy rhythm and waited for him to follow, the others laughing and listening to this new player and Nyssa's challenge. Donal led her into a lament he and Colin had played years ago called "Mother's Grief." Eyebrows cocked, Nyssa followed. How did this stranger know the old music? She'd never heard a bass tuned so cleanly to her fiddle, the throb a perfect octave or two or three below her. Colin didn't like what he heard. He got up and noisily threw more logs on the fire until it blazed up and everyone moved back, crying for mercy from the heat. He handed Danny his spoons and the bottle. Danny called for "My Dungannon Sweetheart," sang and beat out the rhythm. Nyssa played and Donal joined with a simple bass line. Danny tipped backwards off his chair, one leg snapping, and everyone laughed. Marta twisted unsteadily and said to Dagmar, I better go.

She rolled to her knees and got up awkwardly, bending over her stomach, the ground beneath her soaking wet. Dagmar pulled a boy away from men who were teasing him into tasting whisky from the bottle and Danny rolled over into the baby's waters and passed out.

The stranger was playing a cadenza no one had ever heard before. He rang out harmonics at the top and deep rumbles at the bottom. The ground gaped from beneath. The shine of the stranger's scars caught the flames and saucy Nyssa listened. Eager for what she felt when she heard this man play, she put her fiddle high on her shoulder and began to answer his sliding tones. He cut his bow deeper into the strings. She found his key and put in a few bars of a traditional strathspey. Colin laughed and called, Now there's a girl, fiddle him down!

Wrapped in the music and the sound of the sea beyond, Nyssa didn't hear her father. But Donal did. He picked up the tempo and played a counterpoint to Nyssa's tune. She smiled and broke into a reel to see if he would follow. He did and she gave him the solo. He leaned into the strangeness of playing among these people again, his tones travelling over the bare rock toward the shore. He listened to Nyssa, their two minds entwined, the perfectly matching vibrations of their strings deafening their ears. Donal had never heard a fiddler like this girl. She understood his intonation and played into it. He broke out of the reel with a phrase from Bottesini's "Reverie," forcing her finally to drop her bow and listen to him. This music was formal, restrained and unfamiliar. She stood silenced, listening to the hooded hidden figure, his mask pressed against the neck of his instrument, his arms embracing its body but leaning toward her, playing for her.

From across the field, halfway to the house, Marta called out, Someone!

At the strained tone in her voice, the group tore itself from the heat of the fire and the music and hurried over the dark field. Dagmar found her near the greenhouse.

Sweet mother, said Dagmar, She's in labour! Why didn't you say anything?

Marta wrapped her arms around herself and groaned.

Take the children up to the house, said Norea.

Colin said, Let's get her inside. Help me carry her.

The girl shook her head and leaned back. In the darkness Dagmar spread her legs to look. Norea bent down on her old knees and slipped in behind to cradle her head. A hen carried far is heavy, Norea said, wiping the young woman's forehead with her veined hands. We're here.

She's not going to wait for any walk to the house, said Dagmar.

She can't have her baby in a bawn, said Colin.

The girl moaned, rolled to one side and Dagmar and Norea settled into the dirt to work.

Colin put his quilt under her legs and whispered into Dagmar's ear, reeking of whisky, Can you do this?

All she could see was the blood-swollen hole in front of her, the head already pushing through. She hissed back at Colin, You're drunk. If you drop this baby, I'll rip your head off your shoulders. I could use some light.

Colin said, Why would I drop my own grandchild? He squatted beside her, lit a match and held it low.

Dagmar eased her fingers into the hole to massage it open. The girl screamed, Stop!

Norea said low and urgent into her ear, The baby's almost here. Push.

She pushed then and screamed and buoyant Colin raised his match and said, That's it, not a thing to worry about. I saw Danny born. You'll be fine.

Keep that light down, said Dagmar, pulling and stretching evenly. The girl screamed and pushed again. She rested and Dagmar said to Colin, Saw him born! Is that the story you tell? He never laid eyes on him till he was three months old or more.

Norea whispered, Push hard this time, right down, like you're going to shit. You have to get this baby out.

Dagmar reached in to guide out the head, pulling and easing it earthward. She said, You're almost there. Wait. Now . . . breathe and push. I've got the head. I want the rest.

Norea cradled her and whispered in her ear, Push, you've got to push. You wanted this baby. You don't want it dead.

The cruel thought whispered into her ear made the girl lift her head out of Norea's lap, prop herself up on her elbows and with a groan push so hard that she felt as if all her insides were spilling into the field. For the first time in her life she took up space.

Here he is! said Dagmar. She pulled out the slippery baby and she saw in the light of a single match the squashed head of her grandson, his amazed eyes wide open, his mouth pursed with awe. But it wasn't right, and in the thin light she saw that the baby was turning blue. Hard and urgent she said, Mother, take the baby. The cord.

The powerful flesh was wrapped right round the poor child's neck, turbid mother crying, What's wrong! Dagmar thrust the baby into Norea's firm hands and tried to unhook the cord.

Norea said, Have you got it? Don't strangle it.

Then Dagmar did the only thing she could think of, stretched and broke the cord with her fingers. Blood spurted across her face and over the baby and the mother. Colin said, She's bleeding! And no one had so much as a towel or a piece of string. Dagmar thrust her hand into the vines on the rocks and ripped off a bit, raking her hands on the thorns. She tied off the gushing cord with it and said, Stop screaming. You have a baby boy! Look and see.

Dagmar took the baby back from Norea who held it tight inside her own sweater and she wiped and swaddled it with Colin's shirt against the dawning chill. Then she laid the baby on his mother's breast and placed her arms firmly around them and said, Here he is. Perfect as a boy gets. A couple more pushes now, and we'll get out the afterbirth.

Praise the end of it, said Norea and she pulled her sweater back around her and stroked the exhausted mother's hair and struggled to straighten out her own stiff old legs. The fiddle and double bass from across the field had fallen silent.

Dagmar delivered the placenta and dropped it from her bloody aching hands. The others clamoured, Let us see it, and half carried the young woman and her baby and stiff old Norea back toward the house, already singing again.

Make her juniper tea, Norea said.

He looks like Danny, said one.

Do you think he'll marry now? laughed another, and they sang and joked about groaning cakes and admired the baby and the mother.

Dagmar sank exhausted to the ground, wiping her aching fingers on her coat. Colin loitered behind the others and sat behind her and put his arms around her shoulders until she pushed him off.

Get away, Colin. You're drunk, she said.

So?

Something was bothering her, a double bass and a fiddle gone silent. Where was Nyssa?

She said, Did Nyssa go up to the house?

Colin didn't care. He said, Come here for a minute.

She whirled around and pushed him away. She hated the way he pawed her, his lips all thick and wet when he was drunk.

Donal heard in Nyssa's playing by the fire his own devotion to the sound that hands can wring from strings. She was like an ice-loom at sea, reflecting light along a dark horizon, wind springing up, no sign of real icebergs, only their glow in the distance. Old men knew how to navigate by the moan of the sea and an ice-loom in the air. Ears full of Nyssa, Donal could not distinguish her notes from his. Now no other fiddle would do. No one but Nyssa. Her song or nothing.

When everyone headed across the field toward the scream, Donal hit the first rhythmic notes of "Narcissus" for her. She stared at the shrouded figure. Why was he not going with the others?

Donal said from behind his mask, There's enough of them. We'll be in the way. Stay here.

She listened and played back at him, glad to have him to herself, echoing his tunes until finally Donal wrapped his bass into its old case and leaned it like a weary friend against a tree. He stretched out on his quilt to listen to Nyssa fiddle. The field was little changed, Dagmar's greenhouse full. The cool island air shot through him. He breathed in the scent of lichen on the rocky shore. He saw ancient and stunted pines growing out over the breakers.

Nyssa played him some Tartini to show off, and when she was done she loosened her bow and laid her violin aside. She untied her hair and let it fall in a red tumble over her neck and sat near him.

You can play, he said, and then he propped himself up and ran his finger lightly down her forearm.

What are you doing? she said and she didn't draw away.

Strong. Your hands. Your arms. Has anyone told you how soft the skin is here?

She looked down, seeing her own body for the first time. She let him stroke the skin on the inside of her wrist and traced the scars on his hands with her forefinger.

Heave up! she said suddenly, his taut scar tissue under her curious touch. Take off your mask. I want to see your face.

You are original and not timid, he said. She spoke with more self-anointed authority than he remembered in these island women. Used to getting her way. He took her left hand, guided it under the hood toward his lips, kissed the tips of each finger. She closed her eyes and he moved her other hand through the opening at the front of his shirt, brushing her palm against the hair on his chest. He felt her strong fingers break free from his hand to follow their own trails. He slowed himself, lay back and waited until she slid toward him, lifted the edge of his hood. He paused for breath, and buried himself in her strong shoulder and the scent of her skin. She pulled up his hood to glimpse a face darkened by years in the sun, his straw hair and tremulous eyes. She was interested and she opened her own shirt for his surprised lips to kiss her breasts. He eased his arm under her shoulders to shield her back from earth's dampness, his bow hand and lips caressing her. In the tumid darkness he ran his finger along her forehead and saw the little crown-shaped mark at her hairline. He filled her ear with the roar of his breath. From her firm muscles, willingly she took the lead from him *due corde*. She wondered at this strange feeling of wanting him as she wanted herself.

Dagmar stood covered in blood and dirt, thin hair hanging lank around her face, dark-smudged eyes judging and condemning. Nyssa looked into those eyes familiar as her own and rose with lingering lithesome grace, pulled closed her shirt and forgot her fiddle on the ground. She ran across the field toward home.

Dagmar walked to the other side of the fire, picked up the water bucket and dumped it over Danny, who still lay passed out beside the dying embers. She touched her foot to his thigh and said, Fine thing. You've just made me a grandmother. You'd better get up!

He stirred in the dirt. Uncertainly he looked around and said, Wha'?

Your son was just born. They're all at the house. And she pushed him again and said, Get up there and help.

The words slowly penetrated his soggy mind and his long legs loped over the field, carrying him upright out of sheer will, the Nolan in him propelling him toward new life.

Donal stood and for the first time in all those years Dagmar looked into his eyes. He broke her silence.

She looks a lot like you did, Dagmar.

A white-throated sparrow trilled four notes. Grey light. Dagmar raised her chin and said, Leave her alone—you're too old for her. She studied his eyes. He was thicker and more powerful than he had been as a boy. He inhabited his own skin as he had not before.

She said, You can't come back here like this. You can't do this. I won't let you.

He got up from the ground and said, How much longer should I have waited, Dagmar, before I came home?

You took to your scrapers and left. It is too late.

Not too late. I am back.

Words like open husks.

She said fiercely, It's not. Go away. With my bare hands I'll hurt you if you go near her again. Leave her be. She's young.

From his thick height he smiled. Nothing waits. You didn't. I left and you went on. Isn't that how it goes? I'm young still too. I like the way she plays.

A brutal grief seized her heart. She lashed out against him. I tried to play with you. I sat with you. You didn't say a word. You turned away. How was I to know you cared?

I thought you knew. But you didn't play like she does.

He kicked the pant-leg mask into the ashes of the fire, turned his back on her, left Colin's double bass and walked away past the farmhouse toward his sister's house. Lights flickered in every window of Dagmar's rooms. Young people clattered early morning breakfast things, sang songs for the new mother and baby, bickered together comfortably.

In the morning Norea nudged a sooty shearwater lying dead outside the door to her balcony. She crouched over it and spread out and stroked the delicate and powerful wings that could drop into the trough of a wave and slide over its crest without wetting a feather's tip. Broken neck.

Nana, said Nyssa, coming through the door, what happened to that hagdown? I'm in love.

He's dead, said Norea.

How? said Nyssa.

Harbingers of bad weather, said Norea. But that's when they're alive. Does it have a graceful eye?

I guess, said Nyssa. It's only a seabird.

Norea said, Forget the spirit and it dies.

She felt a tear slip down her bevelled skin and was careful to wipe it away.

Norea turned the bird over in her stiff hands. Patiently Nyssa watched her stroke the feathers, and finally Norea raised her head. You're in love, then? I'll have to bury this poor thing.

Yes, said the girl. His eyes are light in darkness, his hands strong and scarred, his music fills me as if it were my own.

You've fallen hard, said the old woman. Don't break your neck!

Nyssa laughed and said, You know, don't you? I think I'd die for him.

I know you wouldn't. We die and are worm food but not for love.

Norea ran her fingers over the spine of the little bird, tried to remember how they looked soaring and dipping down hard on the dories to steal bait from trawls. She sang,

> One evening last week I walked down by yon bush,
> I heard two birds singing—a blackbird and thrush;
> I asked them the reason they sang in such glee,
> And the answer they gave, they were single and free.

Come with me, Nyssa, she said. Help me bury this little soul. It's a dread woman who wouldn't dignify a bird with a proper burial.

Norea chose a place, in the middle of a freshly cleared field, far from her row of bird graves. Nyssa dug the hole while Norea chanted over the open earth. Then she instructed Nyssa to roll large stones to the spot to make a cairn to mark the grave.

Dagmar hurried out from the house, hair still uncombed from the night before. What are you doing? she asked.

Burying my bird, and I'm making a cairn over him.

You can't build a cairn here. I'm using this field next year!

I guess you won't be planting here because I am building a cairn.

Without another word the old woman dropped the stone she was holding, turned and tapped her way across the field for another.

There's hardly earth enough for potatoes on this forsaken island and you're making a bird graveyard! said Dagmar.

Norea kept on walking.

The ragged harbour was unmoved by Norea's labour with stones. She shaped an oval enclosure over the grave. Inside she formed a round circle like a head, a long oval for a body and two stone legs with a little passage between them. Seen from above, the cairn looked like a woman's body stretched out on the ground, measured about ten feet long and five feet across. She sang,

> *Lù ò ra hiù ò*
> *o hì o hì ò*
> *Lù ò ra hiù ò.*

Norea was so thin now that she seemed to disappear between the cracks in the rocks. Nyssa pushed stones until her arms ached and she absorbed the words of her grandmother's chanting, which she did not understand, and the tunes, which she did. All day as she heaved the stones, she thought of the touch of the stranger's tongue between her fingers, the shine of his eyes behind the mask.

Nana, asked Nyssa, have you ever felt as if you were falling with your feet still planted on the ground?

The old woman stepped out from between two rocks and said, I'll soon fall into the honey pot.

What honey pot, Nana?

Death, grave Nyssa, and I'll thank you to bury me here beside my bird and see that your mother doesn't turn this into a planting field.

You can't die for a hagdown Nana, said Nyssa alarmed. There've been plenty of birds die.

And what would be a better reason? Is there a finer life than a seabird's?

Norea got up, walked into the deepest part of the cairn and knelt stiff as an old doll. She said, There is no more leaping for me on these old legs.

Her papery hands were cut to bleeding by the sharp rocks, the earth under her fingernails black. Nyssa came close to help but Norea pushed her aside. No. It is not yet your turn.

So Nyssa squatted and watched Norea reach under her skirt and pull out a small clay axe shaped into the form of a flattened hourglass. Etched on each side of the double head of the axe was the tiny face of an owl, with birds' claws reaching down from the eyes. Norea laid it on her right hand and held it out to Nyssa.

This is for you.

What is it, Nana?

An axe.

What for?

The old woman smiled, her face a ploughed bawn of wrinkles, her yellow hat framing light eyes, the invisible revealed in the visible.

Nyssa frowned. She ran the side of the little axe on her face and looked at the owl's expressionless face, the two ribbons of graven tears streaming down from the eyes.

What does a clay axe do? she asked again.

Cuts, Nyssa. You cut off one life to begin another.

The girl swung the clay axe through the air, fighting an imaginary battle. She ran around the cairn, her axe high above her head, and made Norea laugh. Then she came back to the old woman and she scraped out a hole in the head of the cairn. She placed the little axe in the hole, threw earth over it and stamped the ground down hard. Now I'll always know where it is, she said.

It was clear to Nyssa that her nana was disappearing. Her tear ducts were loose and dripping salt oceans, her hair was falling out limp as mulch straw, her fingernails were yellowing like old leaves, and dark patches of bruise spread under her skin at a touch.

Norea said into her silence, What's the matter?

You look as if you're turning into dirt, said Nyssa.

She rubbed her eyes and took up the girl's hands in her old bony claw. She said, No. Honey. Do you see the bird on my shoulder?

Nyssa looked but she could no longer see. Nana had always said to her when they played, There's plenty of time.

But there wasn't. Childhood is fleeting as the blue flax flower. And stains forever.

Donal tucked a note into Nyssa's violin case beside the fire pit.

> Dear Nyssa,
> Don't ask for reason. You are more eternal than death. I have nothing to wait for but you. Meet me at the stone man tonight.

With singing eyes Nyssa found the note and swallowed his script's umbels and twists. She picked open a seam of the velvet lining at the bottom of her case and hid the note. At dusk she left Norea's cairn and took the path through the woods toward the shore.

Girl, called Moll.

Nyssa looked around and couldn't see her. The voice seemed to come from both up on the gaze and down on the shore. She pretended she didn't hear. She had no taste for Moll today.

You're on whelping ice drifting out to sea, said Moll.

Nyssa said into the air, I'll come tomorrow.

Moll's too stark, she thought. She walked a few more steps and there on the path was the hulked form of a dying deer.

Moll squatted over it. The animal's eyes rolled back and it wheezed for breath. On the side of its long neck was a huge growth that was slowly, inevitably, cutting off its breath. Moll stroked it.

Nyssa caught her breath at the animal's suffering. What can we do? she said.

Nothing, said Moll.

Agony has gradations. But it is no more possible to contemplate the horrible dying of this creature than it is to rest the mind on the hacking off of the limbs of a despised tribe or to see the twisting of a man's body under a beam fallen in a sudden earthquake. All is in the same region of sorrow. The cruelty we bathe in and ignore each day is a part of wisdom that we dare not contemplate for fear of becoming monstrous. It is human to turn away, to cover the eyes, the mouth. But to risk becoming monstrous is to risk wisdom.

I'm not staying, said Nyssa.

Moll did not answer. She would wait. She wanted the deer's bone to skin and dry and use to play her kettle.

Donal waited on the eastern shore behind the pile of rocks, then stepped out in front of her. Nyssa crossed her arms and said to him coolly as if she were performing on stage, I like your playing.

I just scratch, he answered.

Not bad scratching, she said.

Will you come with me?

You think you can just . . . ? She laughed and nodded at his hands. Where'd the scars come from?

She was neither so skinny nor so dewy as he had thought in the darkness. She clambered along the rough shore like any island child. A force and directness was at work in her.

Snakes, he said.

She thought he looked different. He was larger and much older. Without the muffle of his mask she could make out in his speech a remnant echo of the island lilt. The notes of his bass still rang deep in her ears.

Where from?

Have you ever heard a perfect echo? he answered.

He led her to a fissure in the rocks and swung himself up and disappeared into a little cave inside. His hand reached down for her.

Grab hold of that starrigan there, he said.

She grasped the trunk of the gnarled fir tree growing out of the rock, tested it, swung sideways, taking his hand for the final scramble up. She crouched into the gloom beside him and listened to the hush, hush of waves below. He purled a note from deep in his throat.

Nyssa could shiver and scrape and squeak notes. She could hit their singular vibrating centres. She said, The perfect note is when the bow lifts off the string. I have heard sound that makes my eardrums ring.

Donal sang into the cave's mossy darkness, ah and ah and ah on different tones, each echo ringing over the one before.

Then he stroked the soft skin on her forearm and said, You are the condition of music.

Nyssa experienced for the first time (for there is only one first time) the vertigo of passion, the first desire of a girl's stirred-up mind and thighs. The scent of him threw her off and his touch threw her off and his snake-eaten hand reaching to her face threw her off and his tongue against her tongue threw her off. This was the short life of first desire. She marvelled and reached out both hands. The earth with its wide ways yawned and firm rock cracked in two. Donal was amazed by her hunger.

Afterwards they crawled out of the cave and lay under the open sky, listening to the water. She stroked the scars on his hands and said, How long will you have me, now that you have had me?

Forever and a day, said Donal, voice clear against dusk's melancholy. He thought, She's got Norea's voice and Dagmar's face.

Say a day, said Nyssa, without the ever.

Donal looked into the sky and said, You don't know waiting or what it is not to speak.

I never not speak, she laughed.

Donal said, Sometimes it is good to be still and say nothing.

Then it is good to be a stump. Why are you sad?

Donal smiled ruefully. I am hungry as the sea for you and could swallow as much. Sometimes experience makes a man sad.

And what is your experience that it makes you so sad?

I have travelled far from home, wandered away from everything I loved. But that is all gone now. Between home and you, it is all a blank.

Nyssa said, A traveller! And in your travels you gave up love.

But from sad experience I gained you.

Experience makes you sad, she mocked. I'd rather be with someone who makes me dance than have your experience make me sad.

Donal smiled then, but only to please her, as if he were a hibernating bear rousing itself from his winter grave. He had to persuade her.

Come away with me, he said.

And what would I do?

Live with me. I'm only a row across the water. Come, play with me something more nearly perfect.

Thoughtfully she tugged her shirt over her head. Why away? And what was this perfection?

She could not imagine what was across the water, for she had never been off the island. She wanted to go.

All right, she said with a light kiss on his lips, her fingers caressing the insides of his elbows. We'll go tonight. But first I'm playing at the pole house. We'll go after.

PART THREE

SHE
OPENED THE DOOR
FOR HIM

Moll walked through the people of the settlement gathered at the pole house and stood before a ship's lantern. Its light sparked off her bones like a hammer hitting the anvil.

What song have you got for us, then, Moll? said Colin to break the wary and fearful silence.

Moll looked up. She raised her arms to the sky like a bird lifting its wings, wrapped them to the back of her and touched their palms facing upward.

Bring my kettle, said Moll to a young boy standing at the back.

He pushed forward with the pot and placed it at Moll's feet. She unwrapped her hands from behind her back. Her blank black eyes hung there. She took a long bone out from under her dress and began to run it around the rim of the pot. A low echoing moan rose from the pot. She changed the weight and speed of her turning, and the unearthly pitch slid along the one long unbroken note.

Dolente and *dolce*, something inside fulfilling fate. Nyssa stood at the front and listened and doubted and did not find doubt strange. Fingers on the strings. She thought, I have heard what you hear and glimpsed what lies under your dress and the things you do to yourself in darkness. Why do I stand silent with these people full of fear?

She picked up her fiddle and laid her strong first finger across the strings. She grazed her third finger above the second string and played a soft harmonic along with Moll's kettle. The bony woman did not look up but increased her tempo, the sound becoming higher and rounder, and Nyssa followed her, grazing her fingers along the short strings, making little bell tones. Her tones were a fleeting thing over the long drone of the pot. Moll slowed and the pitch dropped. Her eyes stared into its vibrating centre and then she spoke to all gathered there at the pole house.

Below the sea, she said, her hand tracing the pot's compass, is the fathomless one. It sees from the front and back and has twin mouths. It blows with both mouths and spins whoever it encounters so hard that they disappear if they are too afraid to look it in the face. But if they do, its twin mouths turn toward each other and it looks into its other half and goes away. Whoever sees the other half of themselves perishes, or rises out of the dark, peeled naked and new.

She lowered her blank gaze to watch her own hands on the pot.

Listen, she continued, and do not speak. Hear the song of what was lost and washed up on your shores.

And then her words trailed off and the moaning of the pot filled those people like the sound of a storm gathering over the sea. They waited and watched her hand slow and heard the sound fade away. They watched her rise, drop her pot down to her side and disappear toward the sea, which mis-uses nothing because it values nothing.

The Millstone Nether people hung back, afraid of her as they would be afraid of an injured wild creature that might rise up without warning and inflict on them unheard suffer-ing. All remained silent against the night noises, waiting for her to be far away until finally Nyssa lifted her fiddle again, raised her bow, stamped her foot and broke into the first reel of "Nana's Boots." Slowly the others picked up their fiddles and guitars and joined her. By the time Donal arrived late with Colin's old double bass, Nyssa was centre stage, the others laughing and drinking and calling out for more.

He stood at the back and watched. He wanted to peel the jeans from her thighs and unwrap the shirt from her breasts. He wanted to pull her lips to his with the roots of her hair. He thought, How charged she is. But she is still home and far from me.

Shoulders bare, she fiddled, her taut muscles lit by ship's lanterns and white birch skin at night. The Millstone Nether people leaned listening against the sharp air of a hard spring. Music distracted their ears away from the sea, winnowed through the forest, across the bawns and into the open win-dows of their houses on stilts.

Nyssa spun, bore down to centre stage, augered flight, pumped out jigs and reels, the muscles of her back alive. Young people danced and disappeared into the woods in pairs to make love and drink and smoke. When they returned she was still up there, naked under her clothes, stepping and strutting and flirting with the home folk, playing her music fiercely as someone who would not be in this beloved place again.

When the other musicians sat down to rest, she pulled a high stool to centre stage, a black reed in thin light, and opened her ear to the life of her horsehair and sheepgut. She played Tartini's "Devil's Sonata," unravelling its weft as if the notes were a song at a milling frolic. She took up the lightning bowing of its "Siciliano," unable to keep from stamping her foot, her attention so deep inside that the people left listening feared for her return.

All her thought was lost in the music when she was tugged back by Donal climbing uninvited up on stage. With one arched eyebrow she watched him set his bass, its scroll curved over his head, his arm wrapped round its body. She hit the first note of the *moto perpetuo* and he took a deep breath and lifted his bow and played a first note with her. His intonation was so perfectly matched to her own that she felt it through the wooden floor before she heard it. He created harmonies that Tartini did not write. She swung sideways on her stool to face him, closed her eyes, her kinked hair falling forward and hiding her bare shoulders from the people as she began the final and difficult trill. Tenderly Donal faded his deep harmonics while her strings soared and sang, and though he still played, his sound was lost to all but her, as if his bass were being slowly swallowed to death by her little fiddle. And when her last plucked note was gone the people sighed and wanted more.

She cannot bear for long her baroque, he thought correctly, watching her.

Not to disappoint, Nyssa whooped, tossed back her hair and jumped off her stool, knocking it over, stamped and hit the first bars of "Sandy McIntyre." A half smile twisted Donal's lips as he and Nyssa took up again the traditional tunes.

One of the boys pulled her stool to the side and she danced, whirled and spun, away from Donal, back to Donal, so close he could smell the varnish on her fiddle. She dipped its neck down, grazed the air around his fingers, and stepped back, beckoning him with her eyes, knowing he was held fast by his bass like an old dory tossing at anchor. He joined her rhythm and slowed it down, insisting now on his own time. He knew waiting. His eyes locked into hers. He leaned toward her as far as he could without losing his bass in a crash on the stage. He soothed himself, caressed its warm wood with his cheek, the smell of her rosin hanging in the air. Strands of horsehair were snapping and flying loose and slow, casualties fallen into the insignificance of silence.

Colin heard their music echo down from the pole house into the windows of his little place where he'd gone for more spruce beer. He heard the familiar throb of Donal's bass, his daughter's fiddle, playing "Òran do Ghille a Chaidh a Bhàthadh," "Réel Béatrice" and "Close to the Floor." Tempo, key and melody; they changed as one. Nyssa and Donal played and listened only to each other.

The people of the settlement heard the gulf between musician and listener undone. Music vibrated through the sinews and pulsed through the bowels, in the bones, in the blood.

Donal sucked deep the pine air, searched for something she would not know, slid into the first swaying notes of a dancey beguine from "Sonatina Tropicale," teasing her, hamming up the high notes, thrumming a hip-swaying rhythm. He wanted her to listen, but she was never silent. After a few bars she tucked her fiddle under her chin, plucked out the melody and sashayed moonily toward him. The settlement people laughed, and not to upstage the beloved daughter, he gave her the solo. She took it. She stamped the heel of her black boot, stepped beyond his reach. She slowed it down as if she had been given a new power and was sailing away with it. She winked at the people as if to say, Just watch me! She danced across the stage, turned her back and let a lantern's light glance off her red curls. Donal lifted his double bass, walked three steps toward the light beside her, picked up her tune again, in another key, at the very bottom of his register, the only place she couldn't compete with him. He too knew the home crowd. Everyone laughed. Nyssa smiled broadly at his cunning. He was outperforming her but only for her. One last time she lifted her fiddle and echoed back his notes two octaves above until, his head bowed and her neck damp, they touched together the cadenza's last note.

The old people knew that what they heard portended nothing easy but still they willed her back to him. They clapped and called out. Nyssa grinned and rocked on her heels beside Donal.

Eyebrow cocked she said to him between unparted teeth,
What makes you think you can barge in?

That set was *basso obbligato*, he answered. They want more.

They always do. How do you know our music?

Do you give them more? he said.

I don't owe them, she said.

They owe you, he answered.

The people clapped and Donal whispered, I'll be by my
skiff on the shore.

Nyssa dangled her fiddle loosely by its scroll over one
shoulder, her face open as a piece of bare rock and she
answered without moving her lips, Maybe.

And then she handed her fiddle across to one of the boys
on the stage and gestured another to take away Donal's bass.
She stamped, one, two. Again she stamped, one, two, three.
She slapped her hands on her thighs, danced over to him,
took his hands, placed them palms up and outstretched
toward her and used them for her drum. Feet moving, hands
clapping, she beat out one of those old dances that the young
girls did alone in the woods. Her shadows glanced off Donal's
still form and she gestured the girls to come join her and they
did, rising and dancing and clapping in a great web around
Donal. A few fiddlers joined in to accompany the wild dance
until it was all so fast that even those extraordinary musicians
of Millstone Nether could not keep up and everyone fell back
panting and laughing. The old people were tired and began to
drift away home and the young people left in twos, and more
than one young couple tried out love for the first time that
night, alight with the music of Donal and Nyssa. While they

heaved in the forest, the musicians tidied up.

Donal loosened his bow. Nyssa tucked her fiddle into her case, slung it over her shoulder across her breasts. She twisted her wild hair into a knot, baring her long neck. Then she ran lightly on her toes down the path. He knew the path she was taking. She'd walk through the woods and then turn either back to the settlement or along the shore and northward. Donal watched her turn to see if he would follow.

Dagmar lay awake waiting for Nyssa. She listened for her to come through the door, take off her boots and pour a drink of her nana's whisky. She waited for her to shed her clothes by the bed. She waited for her to climb in and slip one leg over her mother's as she'd done since she was a baby, waiting for her old lullaby.

> Loola loola loola loola bye bye
> In your momma's arms a creepin'
> soon you'll be a sleepin'
> loola loola loola loola bye.

Dagmar waited and waited.

Donal had built his rooms on stilts on a bit of shore an hour's row on a civil sea north off the coast of

Millstone Nether. The water rose and fell. It was a studded house, stogged with dry mosses, shingled and clapboarded, dry and safe from winds. He had made two small rooms and a third larger room that served for his living, cooking and eating. He moved his double bass into one of the small rooms. His hands had stiffened with snake-bite. He had bathed them in seaweed and wrapped them with spruce and brown paper.

He had hesitated to go back to Millstone Nether, which he could see on a clear day. He had explored his rough deserted shore through two seasons. He had watched the sooty fog-birds skimming the surface of the ocean and listened for the tiny striped-heads in the trees of the forest behind with their trilling oo-ee-ee-ee-eeee. Most days his horizon was all water. Close enough, he thought, and far enough. A line to be followed.

Now the willing young woman carrying nothing but her fiddle met him at his dory moored and waiting. He jumped in and reached up for her fiddle, tucked it up in the bow safe from the salt damp. She slid into the skiff and headed for the bow seat by her fiddle. But Donal reached for her and settled her between his legs on the middle seat. Reaching around her reed body he placed his hands on the oars and she put her hands on his, leaning back against his chest when he rowed, opening her arms and leaning forward when he lifted the oars out to skim the surface of the waters. He tucked his head into her hair, her hands slipping down to his thighs. He said, Watch the sky for me and keep us straight. Stars hung above them as they steadily covered the expanse of water, Millstone Nether shrinking before their eyes.

When the skiff rocked against the first shallows of the mainland, Donal pulled in the oars, jumped out and pulled the wooden boat up the shore. No wharf to protect it. He tied the dory firmly on an old pine tree, then he held out his hand to help Nyssa who stood, fiddle across her back, ready to leap. She waved him away and flew through the air, toes slipping on the shore stones and falling lightly forward.

Donal led the way through the darkness along the short narrow path, birch trees luminous against the black sea. At the end stood his ramshackle house, stilts stained by the water's ebb and flow. By the door, Nyssa turned him around to kiss her and they pressed together in the stitched light and darkness of their journey.

Donal pushed open the outside door into the larger room with windows overlooking the coast, nothing on the roughly hewn chinked walls. He led Nyssa through another door into a plain room where his bass sat in front of a music stand. He waited silently as she fingered his piles of scores. She opened a notebook full of drawings of birds, anatomies of snakes and reptiles. Neat sketches of dying things. She flipped through it curiously, left it out and open and looked at the music on his stand black with his own notations.

He said, There is another room.

She followed him back into the front room into a small room furnished with a table. The window looked into the cliffs and a thick stand of trees.

He said, This could be your room. Put your fiddle here.

She turned to him and said gravely, Thank you. I have never been given such a gift.

He wanted to take her to the bed in the big room but felt closed in under his own roof.

He said formally, Would you like to look at the sky?

Together they retreated outside again, up into the woods where he'd worn a path to a place silent and still and higher than any other spot on that ragged edge of glacial rock. In the grey dawn she turned to him willingly and slipped off his clothes and pulled him to the ground to make love under a sky growing smurry.

They might have dozed outside all through the morning, but the air grew sharply cold and a strange freezing rain woke them as they dozed in the roots of the gnarled firs. Lovers care little for weather. They rose and gathered up their clothes helter-skelter. Her hand taking his, they flew down the path into the shelter of the house. Laughing they dried themselves and warmed themselves against each other's skin, covered for the first time by the strangeness of sheets, and finally fell asleep.

Dagmar opened her eyes after the restless night and saw a white flower plucked low on the stem, wake robins they'd called them when she was a girl. She looked at the graceful whorl of stalkless greenery, the solitary white bloom. Nyssa had put it in a glass on her night table before she left for the pole house. Dagmar reached to her side of the bed to poke her daughter awake but felt nothing.

She got up and pulled on her gardening pants and shirt. She put on the kettle to boil and dropped tea in the teapot. She opened the door to look at the sky and saw Norea already on her balcony above the apple tree.

What time did Nyssa come in? she called up.

Good morning, Dag.

When she wakes up, tell her I'm in the greenhouse. You want tea up there?

I heard souls slipping under the sea at dawn, croaked Norea.

No, Dagmar thought, and then a chill breeze. Isn't she in your bed?

Norea shook her head.

Didn't Nyssa come home last night?

We didn't bury her shoes.

The kettle screamed.

Time slowed. Dagmar searched the house and Norea's outside loft. The whole house empty. She ran through the greenhouse and shivered with the outside temperature dropping. She headed for the field.

Flax is a clean-up crop. Dagmar sowed hers in rotations. The Millstone Nether soil wasn't suited to it but she liked the seeds and its brief lake of blue blooms, so she nurtured it with all her force. She walked into her unsuitable garden. The flax green was just through, ungrown sepals and anthers still hiding their hint of blue. She plunged into the rows. No dry brown bolls for these—she'd murder them.

Nyssa was gone.

Her little flax field was strewn with old chopped chaff. She pulled and trampled down one row, then another. She stripped away the delicate leaves until her hands bled. She dug out the precious roots. She flung them away and tramped into the next row. She ripped stems and spat into the ground. She would raze it all and leave a swallowing field of stone. She thrashed along until she was exhausted, then she walked down to Colin's to tell him that Nyssa was gone.

Tumbly sea, deep grey swells crashing against the cold rock. Colin spoke from the blasphemy of knowing, She's not a child, Dag. She's got a right to go.

Dagmar raged back at him, She was taken.

She wanted to claw ragged blood rivers through his face. She wanted to scar him with her trowel. She wanted to put seeds in his eyes and blind him. She would reason herself free of his law.

Colin answered into her chill eyes, The ocean's made of mothers' tears. The more suddenly a young girl goes, the more she doesn't want to be found. There were portents.

What portents? said Dagmar.

Patterns, he said. She was poised for leaving. Didn't you know? Mothers are sometimes the last.

Dagmar felt her hand stinging his cheek. What did he know about signs?

He grabbed her wrist hard and brought it down between them, startled as he had been for forty years by her strength. He said, It's as it should be and always was.

Had he no fear?

I will not bend to ways that have no meaning for me, she thought. What divine order have I disobeyed?

She spat on the floor between them and left.

At home she said to Norea, not for the first time, The gods will make me kill him.

Norea answered, That is no god speaking. That is your heart. The truth of it is, she's gone.

I refuse that truth.

It is the truth.

Wrong! *That* truth will kill me.

What good is this, Dagmar? She is already gone. It's happened, she's off.

Now they were two old women grieving each for her own daughter.

Norea paused and said quietly, When I used to deliver milk I found all sorts of things just because people told me they were looking. The side of my wagon was taped up with notices. Once I found a lost china teacup not even chipped. Come, we'll send signs across to the north shore. That's sure where he is. If you measure your sorrow by her worth, it will know no end. Come. A girl like Nyssa doesn't disappear. I'll help you bring her back.

Dagmar went into her room and returned mutely in her oldest flowered dress.

Ping.

The icestorm began with a single ice crystal falling on the humid glass of Dagmar's greenhouse and melting. A drop dripping harmless. And then another.

Ping.

The people of Millstone Nether lay in their beds, listening to the beginning of the storm. Spring-winter, they thought sleepily and pulled up the covers against the temperatures strangely dropping. Late-March storms—they'd weathered plenty of these springs. Capricious crystals. Over the ocean strange ice-snow swirled onto the shore.

When the old people awoke next morning, rooms cold, snow falling with ice, they said, resigned to the weather, Well, the old lady's picking her goose again. They called the snow dung mixen and watched the darkened world already lightly glazed with ice as if caught in the stare of a fevered eye. Transparent sleeves of ice covered young leaf buds and swish ice formed in the shallow water along the shore, tinkling like broken glass. Day deepened again and harder the ice rain fell, layer upon mottled layer, an effervescent icy cataract covering the island. One unique crystal at a time.

Ping.

Norea and Dagmar walked through the storm and gave pictures of Nyssa's face with words scrawled below to sailors hurrying away from the rising storm. They asked the men from away to put them up on the north shore where a girl might see them. Moved by the two old women huddled under thick coats, the sailors took their signs and tacked them up on the other side of the great river. The winds ripped at them and bits of Nyssa fluttered over all the region. The girl with all that red hair smiling, her fiddle under her chin. Bits of Nyssa everywhere. Common as a fallen leaf.

Ping.

At first, people huddled together against the storm as they always did, defying pressures. The first to suffer were the very old. Papery skin and tired hearts, they huddled over kerosene lamps and camp stoves. Arms aching, women kept small babies in slings against their own skin, wrapped warm against the storm.

Ping.

At Dagmar's the branches of the stiff old pine behind the greenhouse sagged with heavy glistening ice. A marvel. Each needle was wrapped in shining ice, each cone shining with frozen ice. It thickened in layers on branches that squeaked and cracked and finally crashed down under the weight. Branches fell away from the trunk in long reluctant tears until the whole tree cracked and broke and smashed the green-house with a spectacular crash in the freezing wind. Shattered glass mingled with ice in heaps of shards around crumpled green piles of plants and tomato seedlings. Glass sliced through rows of Dagmar's indigo pansies freaked with jet, luminous for a few hours under the frozen leaves. Tumid ice branches fell and lay freezing on the earth. Dagmar's radiant and difficult pink bougainvilleas, even her *opuntia compressa* with its yellow prickly pears could not withstand the rubble of ice and glass. She wrapped her apple trees with thick rags. She kept Norea's outside loft heated with the wood fireplace and they cooked on the Rayburn in the kitchen. She stood with Norea on the porch, watching winter grasses creak and sway. They talked about Nyssa and bet matchsticks on which dangling leaf would next twist and crack and fall.

In the torment of absence Dagmar imagined Nyssa's hair, her music, her wide grin, her green eyes. Gone. Habits of sound, of encounter, of love. Gone. With each ticking minute Dagmar was slowly broken, ribs cracked, gut cut open, heart slashed raw, lungs punctured. She awoke in the night, thinking what could she do more. Never are we closer to our own godliness than in loss. Reflecting backwards we apprehend unbearably how mortal and limited we are. If only we had thought like gods. The suffering of loss is infinite because we are sure things might have been different if only we could think in the way of eternity.

The people of Millstone Nether clung to their old radios and listened to the crackling voices of ships' weather forecasters who said they'd never seen such strange build-ups of pressure in the early spring. All the buds on the ground bushes were dead and the small hard berries cracked off without getting green. Dagmar wandered her bawn and along the shore, looking across the great river and mourning Nyssa. The dusk drew on, loosing from striving every living thing in all the world save her.

Inside the house she shone for him. He pressed his neck close against hers. They could not get enough of each other. They made love before sleeping, in the night when one or the other was roused by a dream's meander or the body's restlessness, in the morning at first touch. They dragged their instruments from room to room to play together and dropped to the floor to make love. They cooked and ate together and did not know what day it was. When they grew tired of indoors, they bundled up to walk out and look at the relentless freezing ice. Nyssa tucked all of her hair up under an old toque of Donal's and delighted him when she pulled it off in the winds, red kinks and curls tumbling around her face. Stretching, striding, pretending she didn't know how much her hair, her eyes, her touch pleased him. Nyssa said, I never want to go back, and Donal said gravely, You don't have to.

Playful Nyssa imagined new ways not to touch.

Be still, she commanded him one afternoon as they lay naked. He was proud of his well-tuned body and his insatiable fingers tapped his own skin absently. Between kisses Nyssa traced the irresistible curves of his *linea semi-circularis* and said, You're very fit for your age.

Donal lifted his head from the pillow and contemplated his naked fiddler-lover, fingers stroking the soft and moist skin above her breasts firm as snap peas. Why must the body dry? he wondered.

Heedless, quick-tongued Nyssa lifted her lips from his skin, bounced off the bed and said, I'm going to draw you. You're not allowed to move.

She padded into her practice room and brought back a sharp pencil and a stack of discarded staves. Strange how you have nothing to draw on in the house but music paper, she said.

Nyssa threw out her little critiques without thought. She knew no other way to talk. Dagmar and Norea had never censured the girl's stream of chatter. They abided her tactlessness in favour of her truth. Donal lay still by Nyssa's royal command, her detached gaze upon him. She drew. Playfully he reached out to touch her toenails, white chips of moons.

Nyssa said, Stop. Don't move or I'll tear it up and start all over again. She was as absorbed as a child in her new game, tracing the shape of his body onto the page of musical staves.

He acquiesced and lay and watched the outside light diminish, only his eyes allowed to caress her body, the tilt of her neck, the *punto d'arco* of her pretty breasts. He composed in his head the new variations he would perform when at last released to touch his skin to hers.

She did not show him her artwork. She handed him the pad of paper and pencil and told him to draw her. He dashed off a sketch, tossed the paper aside and reached for her.

She said, Not good enough. I want detail. Pretend I'm one of your bird specimens.

He sat up and arranged her body in order to touch her and began to dissect her and draw her. He commenced with her bow hand and by the time he had completed its visible and invisible complexities—twenty-six fine bones in the fingers and wrist, loose joints, fingernails, palm lines boding—the room was completely dark. There was much left to do. Her soft forearm, her muscular upper arm, the crease of her underarm waited undrawn.

Nyssa said, Let me see.

She was surprised when he held up the sketch of her hand. She tossed the pages to the floor and wrapped herself into him in the pure pleasure of self-immolation *à deux*.

They returned over and over to their drawing game. Nyssa's portraits grew more abstract. She worked more in sound than in shape. She rendered Donal's body a thicket of notes on a musical staff, a new musical composition *a cappriccio*. She secretly took her sheets to her practice room to play. Donal dissected her, bit by bit by bit, and tacked his pages to the wall in joined pieces of her portrait, the proportions according to his preferences—a hand the same size as her head, her lovely toes larger than her breasts, the soles of her feet. Nyssa commanded him to make love only to the piece of her he had just drawn, rose and sank in the pleasures he could act upon each lovingly observed morsel of her body.

She favoured the loom of novelty and devised new ways to separate herself from Donal, persuaded that delayed touch was sweeter. Sometimes in the middle of making love she stopped, got out of bed and made him listen to her play her fiddle. Sometimes she commanded him to get up and play *basso buffo* with her. Then they'd start all over again.

On the island of brown tree snakes, only one type of gecko escaped extinction. When it got caught, it peeled itself free of its own skin and left the snake with nothing but a dry bag in its methodical jaws. Donal admired the gecko's cunning. He watched Nyssa as the days passed and it seemed to him that she was peeling off her old skin but he could not say why.

No other animal suffers so much as a frail human fated and drawn by love to the infinite possibility of wisdom. Nyssa was enthralled by Donal's fast devotion to the perils and transcendence of horsehair on sheepgut. He showed her gentle tricks to coax from her violin a sound more pure. He said, You can train your instrument, and he tried to stretch her talent. All notes planted themselves effortlessly in her mind. She looked at scores and discerned their patterns. She preened and stretched like a cat at Donal's unmasked pleasure in her quick ear and nimble fingers. She found intonations that rang together with his, all other sound disappearing from heaven and earth.

But Nyssa grew bored with pitches so perfectly matched. She teased him by sliding up and down around the notes. When he couldn't entice her back, he played harmonics. His long strings rang out in a way her shorter ones could not. He hit the note and ran his finger up the string from the nut without really dampening it. He made a deep, echoing bell tone that punctuated her cheeky dissonance. She listened and was strangely moved by hearing him strut and display what he could do. She watched his great hands seek sounds that might please her, listened to him venture uncomfortably beyond his beloved consonance and felt tender toward him. They played for themselves and for each other. They played and played as one, and sometimes when they finished and the music fell silent, they were astonished and even a little afraid.

They'll be missing me, Nyssa ventured restlessly one twilight, lying on the carpet where they'd dropped head to foot, touching Donal's inner forearm with her toe. How long have I been gone?

Donal traced his lover's foot, ignoring what he feared most from her. He said, kissing the tip of her left baby toe, Let's try the beginning of the "Très Vif" section of the Ravel. He watched her wade into and wend through the difficult piece, concentration alight on her clear forehead over arched eyebrows, admired her tenacity in its unfamiliar terrain.

Perhaps I should send word, she said, withdrawing her toe.

The river is full of ice, he said.

She pulled herself up to her elbows and said, They're old. Nana needs me.

They're fine, answered Donal. There were worse storms before you were born. Stay. I'm old too.

She said, I will scold you for being old before your time.

It is my time, he said.

Then do not be old before you are wise, she answered. Why do you try to stop me from doing what I like?

Don't torment me, he said. Your music has made me complete.

And what of me?

Donal had unfurled in Nyssa a vast wilderness of touch. He left inevitable traces. For the first time she was divided from herself, awake to the frail melancholy of the flesh.

That night she stared out at the ice lace on the window, with a shivering fear of falling. She stamped her foot lightly to recapture herself, raised her hopeful fiddle and played the familiar reels in her "Nana's Boots."

Through the wall Donal searched for ever more intriguing pieces to play together. He showed her Bottesini's "Grand Duo Concertante" as well as the "Passione Amorosa." She felt that Bottesini favoured the bass parts. He gave her Bach's "Chaconne in D" and improvised an accompaniment.

Lying on her back, balancing her fiddle upright on the tips of her fingers, Nyssa said, But it should challenge you as well.

Willingly Donal acquiesced. He looked for a piece that would please them both and pulled out Handel's "Passacaglia." Yes, he thought, its plucking, its romantic interludes, its hard, quick bowing and nimble finger work, yes, it will please her no end. He wandered into her practice room where she lay on the floor listening to "L'arte del arc." She said, I'm busy. You just left.

That's not what I came for. I have found a piece for you and me, and I have a dress for you to perform it in.

She rolled to her side and said, What colour is it?

A surprise, if you'll wait for me.

How long will you be?

All time away from you is an eternity. It is in my room. I'll go now. Will you wait for me?

Home was not home any more. Houses in Millstone Nether burned to the ground in the freezing rain as people tried to warm themselves with lanterns and candles. Some locked their doors for the first time in all the years, afraid. Old people fingered the edges of their blankets. Children cried with cold and no boy challenged another to jump the icebergs.

Norea was confused by the uncanny cold. She could not remember the days of the week or what she ate. She sometimes did not know where she was. She began to talk to Dagmar as if she were still a child. She talked to her own dead mother, forgot that Nyssa was born. She begged her daughter to make the ice stop and Dagmar said, Not until I find Nyssa.

Norea sat in her deep-fetched darkness, wrapped in quilts. When the frozen rain tapped the window she heard the clatter of milk bottles and the cry of her young mother dying. She trenched potatoes until her young arms ached, she shivered frightened across Ireland and lay wretched in the stench of a ship's hold. She slipped eggs in worn grey paper cartons through little doors into the houses of the settlement, and gathered up and buried dead birds. There lay a baby beside a bull. She walked into her first house, holding hands with

Rory, and heard three old sheep-faced women chanting to her the old hauling home song:

Oro, sé do bheatha a bhaile, is fearr liom tu ná
céad bo bainne:
Oro, sé do bheatha a bhaile, thá tu maith le
rátha.

A chill of light hunger distracted her from the bright stream of sound and touch. When she woke up she was disappointed to be in her outside loft, caught in the tedium of aching hips and throbbing hands. She shook memory away from her like a dusting rag and reached reluctantly into the cold from under her blankets, felt for a plain cracker in the dish lying beside her teeth on the bedside table and broke it between her gums. She sucked the cracker until she could wind her old tongue around and gum it into throat-sized gulps. Her water glass was frosted and she wanted hot tea. She thought, Too creak cold to get up. I'll just tuck my head in under here and rest. Oh, but my throat is dry. She pulled her wool hat down over her thin hair and drifted back to her imageless sleep.

For in my mind, of all mankind, I love but you alone. She heard Rory singing "The Nut Brown Maid." Rory, dust to ghost transpeciated. Then she saw him. He stood before her in the frozen room with his disarming grin, hand half raised toward her. She knew she was half aslumber and he dead, yet there he stood. And his voice. She stopped herself from moving for fear of losing him. She watched him raise his other arm toward her, come forward to her. Be still, Norea warned herself, keeping her eyes closed. Don't frighten him away. All his life-lost sadness reached across into a world no longer his. He stepped nearer again, eyes abrim with longing for the young woman throbbing with desire for him and then Norea had to breathe and he was gone. She lay still, trying to bring him back but he was gone and tears rolled unhindered down her old cheeks, burning holes through the cold sheets.

She struggled to sit up in bed. Where was Dagmar? She watched new ballycatter ice freeze in lacy patterns on her windows. She feared the dusk, hours of cold chafe and loneliness. Where was Dagmar? Wasting with desire for her daughter. She struggled to pull her old bird legs out from under the heavy covers to go downstairs in the dark. She had to walk out now. Try to fix things. Hadn't she done it many a time, left her home, hitched up the milk wagon or walked off a worry?

Donal set the yellowed box at Nyssa's feet, the music in his wide pocket, his return post haste to his restless fiddler achieved and she still there.

Open it, he said.

Nyssa lifted the lid and folded back the old shelf paper. She had never had a dress in a box before. She lifted the material and couldn't see which end was which. The bodice had no shoulders and zipped up the side. The skirt fell full and was cut on the bias from a nipped-in waist. Nyssa held it in front of her, then dropped the few ounces of fabric to the floor, slipped out of her familiar jeans and shirt and slithered on her knees into the centre of the dress like a child crawling into a tent. Squatting, she tugged up the bodice until it lay over her breasts and she twisted sideways to do up the zipper. Then she stood in a single motion, swept back her hair and tied it up on itself to reveal her full naked shoulders and back, the skirt clinging silkily to her thin hips and muscular stomach. Donal looked at the smooth skin over her clavicle and admired the round firmness of her upper arms.

Turn around, said Donal.

Wait, said Nyssa. There's something else in the box.

She lifted out a pair of brocade boots in gold and cranberry and blue. She undid sixteen gold ball buttons along their sides and slipped them on her feet with delight.

They'll fit when I do them up, she said, lifting her foot and clacking down the heel.

She reached into the box for the button hook. Slowly she pushed the little curved end inside each button hole and slid it around, looking for the button to pull through with a tiny pop. When she was finally finished, she straightened up and danced, then leaned over again to admire the boots, raised gold threads of swirling leaves wrapped round her ankles and feet.

She twirled, humming a strathspey, lifting up the full skirt and stepping, listening to the clatter of those curved heels, mocking the dress and adoring her boots.

He watched and imagined how the muscles of her back would throb when she was finally persuaded to stand still, to let the fabric hide those peculiar boots, to gravely lift her violin and play. He admired how the silky black cut a straight line under the lovely V that ran from her shoulders to her breasts firm and hidden, her neck's curve fleetingly glimpsed through kinky hair when he asked her to let a few tendrils down. He imagined how she would be angled slightly toward their audience, lift her violin and play. The eyes of strangers would glimpse the nakedness of her arms and back and clavicle, the concentrated tilt of her head and the clarity of her brow. Strangers would hear what he heard and watch what he possessed, music and muscles, sinew and flesh.

The wake-robin Nyssa picked for Dagmar died and hung brown and folded over on the bedside table. Bed mites collected on the leaves' waxy surfaces and the stem shrivelled. The water was dried and gone.

Norea shook her daughter, wrapped up in bed, and said, Dagmar, I've been dreaming of your father.

Mother, he's been dead sixty years, said Dagmar, pulling herself up. I never met the man.

Of course you did. He loved you like you were his own skin. Don't you remember the little deal cradle he made you?

He didn't, Mother. You told me that this morning, and yesterday, snapped Dagmar.

Norea saw the little cradle. Her three youngest brothers had all slept in it. She stopped, perplexed. But stubbornly she said, Of course he did—you just don't remember.

Dagmar saw the blue ridges around Norea's lips. I'm taking you to the school. It's too cold to leave you here.

This is my house and I'll do in it as I please and I won't leave it! With stiff hands Norea swept away the bits of dried petals lying on the table beside Dagmar's bed. If you don't like it, get your own house!

She thrashed at the rest of Nyssa's dead plant and Dagmar snapped, Don't touch that. Don't talk to me like this!

Norea heard the axe edge in her daughter's voice but she could not remember who Dagmar was. With a forest animal's instinct she spat out, Filthy shrine, and knocked the small vase to the floor.

Stop it! Dagmar got out of bed and crossed the room. She looked back and saw the strange old Irish woman mumbling something in a foreign tongue and she sat down and sobbed.

Norea heard her little girl crying and her memory came back again. She went over to her, caressed her head, crooned, Don't carry on. It hurts my eyes to look without seeing you. Then memory flickering back confused, she said, No one can cross the river when it is full of ice. Wait till the melt and then we'll go get her. Let her go, Dag, a girl has to go. You did!

No! raged Dagmar, brushing her old mother's hand away, It is not the same. I never left the island. I could throw a pebble from Colin's house to yours. I hear the throbbing of her voice in the storm. A girl must have a way back.

She left the room, went into the kitchen, threw on her coat and walked outside. Alive, Nyssa had disappeared into darkness. Ice fell and the sky cracked. Dagmar could no longer retrieve the details of Nyssa's nose, her lips, her cheeks. She could not finger her hair or look into her green eyes. She could not smell her or hear the sound of her voice. She could only feel the pain and easing of a baby latching to her breast.

She lamented, Nyssa, my daughter, my dolour. Nyssa child of mine. *Air fàil irìnn ì rirìnn*. Nyssa, where are you? Speak daughter, any tongue. Long-limbed, spinning steps and fiddling fingers, one cocked eyebrow under all that kinked hair, doom-eager. You cannot disappear, free creator of yourself. Earth will stay frozen to its core until my eyes rest on you once more.

Together Donal and Nyssa listened as the ground bass set out the melody of the "Passacaglia" in a stately triple metre, nimbly followed by the violin with its playful polyphonic variations. Fiddle tripping, bass embracing, daa ta daa ta daa ta daa, fiddle dancing, bass leaping, each seizing hold of the other in grace, in delight, in melancholia and teasing. They parted and returned, sometimes sensual, sometimes in strife, playful, grave, tender, restrained and released by form, their two different beings one in the last variation, golden threads made divine in the music until they were torn asunder and rendered silent. Dominant to tonic, Handel's shantih and amen.

Donal marked up the score while Nyssa rested on the floor, hearing the music inside. She rose and traced her finger across the notes, absorbing the sound through her eyes, through her whole naked body. She picked up her violin and picked out bits of its melodies, the witty plucking, the dramatic crescendos. Together they worked through the music, hour after hour, becoming the notes, becoming the dance, their instruments ringing together.

Handel, she sniffed when they were done. I want something fresh. Play that harmonic for me again.

Twenty-five days she'd been gone, she figured by the moon. He talked of concerts on the mainland and of playing for strangers. He wanted her to play her Tartini, and he his Bottesini. He wanted to dress her. He wanted to end with their "Passacaglia." The sounds of these words tripped like precious little chirps from his lips and offended her. What about a set of reels? she had said. He shook his head. Not fancy enough for you? she scoffed. I'll show you what I'll play for them. She lifted her little fiddle under her chin and played a long drone. On top of it three clear harmonics, then she stepped a little dance.

The world will beat a path to our door, he said when she was done, but not for that.

She laughed at him and said, Who cares for the world at the door? When it comes I turn it away.

What do you want, then? he asked.

She stopped, then said, I want to write the music I hear and cannot yet play.

His brow furrowed and he said, And what is this music?

She hesitated. I heard it once when I slipped and fell under an ice pan into the harbour. I've heard it when I'm up on the gaze with Moll. I hear it under pine needles on the rocks.

Moll! He scoffed. What does she know about music? You can play Tartini. Precious few can.

He watched Nyssa's eyes go blank and made himself stop. Then he said, Let's talk about it more later. Come, let's work on our breath.

She relented once again and sat facing him cross-legged, knees dropped loosely on the floor, the palms of her hands resting open on her knees. Stiffer Donal sat hips taut, chin tipped, and showed her elaborate breathing routines he had invented to match the phrasing of the music. Nyssa practised taking short inhalations to mark new phrases.

Don't get involved with your breath, said Donal, but know where it begins and ends.

She let her breath out. She could see her mother's rare flax spreading its ocean of blue blossoms toward the sky.

Donal watched her nostrils go soft and said, Good. The breath holds the tempo, projects the sound.

Annoyed by his intruding talk she stopped suddenly and flung her feet in front of her. I'm sick of this! she said. I'll breathe how I want!

She jumped up, raised her fiddle and played a difficult passage, holding her breath. When she was done, she dropped her violin and said, sucking in air, There!

Donal said, But it didn't ring. Intonation is the most important element of volume and projection. It improves with the breath.

Leave me alone! she said.

Donal reached out to stroke her lovely bowing biceps and the smooth muscles of her thighs. He touched her neck with kisses, whispered apologies, promised not to correct her ever again. He wanted the taste of her salt tears as much as he wanted her other briny flavours. She wondered how the flat emptiness inside had come. She had entered him as a swimmer enters death.

Her body still tingling and wretched she left for her own room. There she rocked on her heels and stared out the window. She examined the astrean light on the trees. Who knows I am not dead? she thought. Does my mother think of me? I am completely lost in him. Smelling the earthy odours of their lovemaking between her legs, she thought, Is this love? No sooner did she sponge him off in tingling ice-melt than he came to find her and they were wrapped together again. My body, she thought with disdain, is a grave that accepts anything. He plays it over and over and over. I despise it and then when I have been away a little I want him again. I am suffocated by him. And freed. She stared into the darkness.

All things in nature have a latent song, things dreaming until a breath gives them voice. The tune in the hollow reed, the echo in the cave. Breath in. Breath out. With each breath, new life.

What time is it? yawned Nyssa.

I am your clock and your season, teased Donal, laying down his tray on the bed.

If you are my clock and season, then I am only a month old and the season is spring. But look out the window, it's cruel ice everywhere.

The better to keep you here wrapped in my arms.

She said, And why would you keep me with ice when you could set me free to fly back to you with love?

Nyssa dumped whisky into her tea and drank it down. She reached for her music pad and wrote in it playfully, then passed it with the pen over to Donal who blew on his coffee.

> Dear Mr. Donal Dob,
>
> I am looking for a future. But all I am interested in are sounds you say are not music. If I can find a future with you, please meet me in five minutes on the south side of the bed. Of course, I will need to know the time!
> > Yours sincerely,
> > Nyssa Nolan
> RSVP (here!)

Donal willingly took the pad. A new game. He picked up the pen and wrote back:

Miss Nyssa,

By what miracle would you be attracted to hoary old me? Reponse: oui. In your monochord there is no melody. What do you see in that awful droning and plinking?

Yrs.,

Donal

P.S. You carry all songs under your tongue.

He handed her the book and pen, slid to the bottom of the bed and Nyssa stood up and shuffle-stepped toward him over the blankets and sheets, hair wild from the night, writing in large loops that filled up the page:

Dear Donal,

You didn't tell me the time. I arrived on the losing of the moon. The sky is dark again. May the angels protect you. Has your mind ever hummed with the twangling of the earth? Why do you find it awful?

Fiddlingly,

Nyssa

She tossed the notebook down beside him. He tried to reach for her ankles but she shook her head, pointing to the pen, a stern finger on her closed lips. Reluctantly he picked up the pad, read and wrote again:

Dear N,

    Harmony in the balance and order of the gener-
ations. Can that be exhausted by such as us?

                Angelically,
                Donal

Nyssa squatted beside him, reading upside down, and grabbed the pen out of his hand as he finished his signature. Then she took the notebook far away to the pillows at the top of the bed, turned the book right side up and read what he wrote. She wrote back:

> Dear Angelic (Good? Bad?) Donal,
>   Even an angel is burdened with wings. You lack valour. I'm tired of never being alone. I am weighed down by musty counterpoint. And I'm tired of you wanting to be always right. And safe.
>
>   N.

Solemnly she handed back the book and he looked up as if to speak. Again she raised her finger to her lips and pointed. Donal knew the fruit of strict obedience to the rules of her games and silently he wrote:

Dear Nyssa,

    I will love you for all eternity. I cannot
account for you playing with equal exquisiteness
all that I give you. I cannot account for you

wanting both me and solitude. I cannot account
for your restlessness or your talent or your taste.

Dear Donal,
    But you can prevent me from achieving
what I want.

Dear Nyssa,
    Let us perform our "Passacaglia." The world
will listen. In time you will feel differently.

Dear Donal,
    You talk of performing when I talk of being
alone. You talk of counterpoint when I think
about bone on metal. Is this what love becomes?

How sinewy her body had grown. How strange
she had become even to herself. Nyssa closed her door and
laid empty staves out on the floor and tried to write. Note
after note after note. She crawled, squatted, sat cross-legged,
leaning over her paper, back cramped, hands sliding the paper
from one side to the next. Only one line of music on each
piece of paper. She played them and threw them aside dissat-
isfied, was strangled by the five lines and four spaces of the
staves, boxed in by the bars, by the treble clefs, weighed down

beneath what she knew had been written before. She wrote from memory. She drew a long score for a prepared piano and crumpled it up. She hummed her Millstone Nether tunes. She worked from the high technique of choice, wilfully limiting herself, wilfully eliminating all that was not hers.

Bewildered and searching she copied out the wordless songs she'd heard her grandmother singing in the cairn. She listened to the melody moving in its narrow range, series of tiny motives growing attached like crystals of ice and building exquisite shapes. Ancient and honoured, melismatic or plain. But even that wasn't what she wanted.

The walls could not hold what she had to say and neither could her old fiddle. Something was consuming her and stopping her from the straightened flame of the hearth. She was driven to write what bullied her insides. Her womb ached. Pain throbbed through her and she pressed her skin against the cold glass of the window.

She wrapped herself up and walked outside along the edge of the rocky cliffs overlooking the sea. She crouched on the frozen ground and chipped a little depression into it. She listened to the winds and the ice and heard inside her all the sounds of Millstone Nether. She forbade Donal to come into her room that night as she played over and over all the harmonics her little fiddle could find. She played them in rhythms like the sound of ice under water. Sound without tune or tradition, thinly awaiting density. In these notes she wished to elaborate pattern, structure, energy, surprise, joy. In these notes she wished to find pitches no one had heard before, waiting like baby spiders to be born. She wanted this.

More than home. More than love. She was fed up with Donal's tiny rooms, his tired music, his plan to perform. She wanted her rhythms that sounded from the darkness and the bottom of the sea. She had to go back.

In the other room she heard Donal running his finger up and down his long strings, changing the pitch on his natural harmonics in a way that she could not on her fiddle. His practice said through the wall, I can do anything.

Donal knocked on her door and pleaded with her, You can't not play with me. We no longer exist apart. Without me, no bass. Without you, no soaring.

She said, That means nothing to me.

Impatiently he dropped his hands and said, There were times on Millstone Nether before the spring of the barrels of instruments when the people were so poor they had no fiddles. I've heard stories of the first kitchen parties where an old man took a piece of board and some string, took sap straight from the trees for rosin and played it. Look at your fiddle. And you don't want to play it?

She mocked him, saying, What a cruel sad story. Scattered few would believe that one.

He laughed then, and he bowed the opening bars of "Narcissus" and she could not prevent her body quickening and she let him pull her to him one last time. But as soon as he was making love with her, *con expressione di patimento,* she became distracted and her mind fingered over a tale her nana used to tell her about the beginning of the world.

A sister and a brother lived together in darkness until one night a stranger lay beside the girl and made love to her. The sister fell asleep and when she awoke the stranger was gone. Next night, again he came, and again he lifted her up, and again, when she awoke, he was gone. Finally she blackened her hands with burned sticks from the fire and when he came in the darkness, she held his face between her palms. Eagerly she went out in the morning hoping to see some sign. But there squatting by the fire was her brother, long finger marks streaking his face. She screamed at him, It is you who had me in darkness. She tore off her breasts and hurled them at him, then picked up a large burning fire stick from the fire and ran away. He picked up a smaller fire stick and ran after her. They ran so fast that they rose up into the sky and caught fire. She became the sun and he the moon chasing over a world newly lit by the sorrow in the darkness.

Donal lifted her hips to his, his eyes closed and lips apart, breathing hard. She watched his face and waited, her mind turning over the story. Donal stroked her lovely linea alba and she looked away, her nana's bodewords chilling: Forget the spirit and it dies.

PART FOUR

WAYS
THAT MAY NOT BE
QUESTIONED

W hen a cycle ends there is an emptying. The old pleasures go lacklustre. The old desires dry up. The cycle sometimes ends with a death, a loss. But sometimes it just ends. There is a call to be somewhere else. That is the truest explanation for the end of one thing and the urge toward another. One thing done, another ready to begin.

He could not stop her. Nyssa had plunged into the sea that silenced minor streams. She was out of sorts and restless, her music a practice for death. She wanted only to search out the unsounded experience. She wandered from wall to wall of her little room. The hours stretched endlessly around her. All sound flat against these wooden walls, webbed in by notes worn out, she baulked and began again the stripping-down. He said when she played that she could make ring all of heaven and earth. But she wanted still another realm. She wanted to reveal what lay hidden below. Nyssa Nolan had leapt fully formed. She wasn't the sort to wither.

Donal brought his double bass into her room and said, Let's play.

No.

Donal slammed his hand on the wall. Where had their sweet love gone? Was silence all? Their love extinct?

Play with me, he said.

Nyssa said, The face is yours. The spirit has fled.

What are you talking about? Listen to reason. The lifelovingest part of him would no longer lie beside him or play with him.

She looked at him and saw a stranger who would not listen to her. Gently she placed her beloved fiddle on the ground, and raising her brocade boot above it, she stomped down hard. The fine old wood cracked in useless splinters, the tailpiece popped off and the strings sprang tangled and slack. One of the pegs popped out and landed away from the smashed wood like a chopped-off finger. Chipped varnish and silent sheepgut lay murdered between them.

His eyes searched hers and he tried *sotto voce*, Let's stop all this. I'll get you another fiddle. If you love me I will always love you. It doesn't matter what you do.

In an instant's compass her heart closed to him.

She said, There is no *if* in love.

She walked past him and her dead fiddle toward the door.

Nyssa scrambled down the shore and untied the dory. The glow of ice-loom across open water. Swish-ice clinked like chains in thousands of little chunks along the shore. Farther out in the strait were deadly ice floes. She thought, He closes the door and my heart sneaks out the window. He closes the window and it sneaks out the chimney. My bearings and balance are not inside those rooms but out beyond.

She saw wrapped round a tree by the shore a scrap of her own face, the paper torn and blown. Across the chin scribbled in her mother's hand was the word *Missing*. Her face torn in two, part of her fiddle tucked under her chin, the rest blown away. The storm was pitching up again in the north. She wanted to get across. She slipped into the middle seat and broke the ice frozen over the oarlocks. She lifted the heavy oars. The old wood was rubbed smooth with the pull of hands and covered in a sheaf of ice. She swung the two long blades against the chunks of ice in the water. The oars sounded like straw thrashed with a stick as they moved heavily through the ice. Facing the direction from which she came, the nose of her boat taking her blindly toward Millstone Nether, she rowed. She was afraid of the swells and of the banquese ice, broken floes drifting down from the north. She tried to make out the stars to keep straight. Night clouds curtained the sky and ocean winds swung her boat around. She pulled and pulled until her own torn face on the shore was a speck. For a long time she pulled, trying to keep the wind at the same angle on her cheek. By midstream, the stars invisible and winds whipping her bow around, she cried out, afraid of the fearsome frozen floes, but the sound reached no ear. She rowed now only to keep her boat from tossing over. I have small chance, she thought. Minutes hours and hours minutes, the time it takes to tend the dying, shrouded with freezing rains she kept pulling only because there was nothing else to do.

After a long time, she felt an opening in the ice floes and the pull of a current as if there were a vessel ahead. She pulled in behind and waked it. She had to trust its pull through the invisible leads and channels. She could make out a dory and in it a figure long-limbed and bony like a shadow puppet moved by thin sticks behind a screen. It pulled her ahead through the darkness. She felt thick shore ice, and she looked over her shoulder and saw the cliffs of Millstone Nether and heard the cracking of tree limbs through the frozen stillness of an island out in the gulf of that great freezing river.

She looked around for the boat she had waked and saw nothing but ice and darkness. She drifted aporetic near the shore, unable to land her dory caught between two icebergs. She brought in her oars and leaned over them, her shoulders aching, and rested her forehead down against the frozen wood. She shed her heavy oilskin. She wanted to lie down and sleep yet roused herself. You can't sleep in this cold, she thought, unless you want to sleep to death. Her strong mind grasped that and clung to it, benumbed in the frozen darkness.

Only one stilt house in the settlement did not suffer greatly in the storm. Madeleine and Everett were accustomed to cold and darkness and thin rations. They endured these things because they had their secure store of paint and tobacco. Madeleine's rocker feet were useless against the ice and Everett took over the cows during the storm. This left her inside. In the first days she painted what she could see from her window: the ice-locked harbour, a branch wrapped in a sleeve of ice, Everett milking a purple cow. She painted the insides of their rooms as she thought of them: an empty chair beside a window, a cat curled up on a brightly squared counterpane, a pot hanging above a hot stove. She painted in the pot's shiny reflection her own chin pulled down into her neck and her webbed elbows. She smiled. She turned to a fresh paper and painted the only self-portrait she ever made. In the middle she outlined a door like any other on Millstone Nether, but in bright reds and blues and without a doorknob. Outside she drew herself, half turned away, her crabbed hand reaching up, unable to open the door but ready to enter. It had to be opened from the other side.

Madeleine put down her paintbrush and blew on her cold hands. She spent the rest of the morning mixing the brightest golds and yellows she could make, and then on the other side of the door she painted Moll.

Nyssa collapsed, slumped and curled up in the bottom of the dory, pellets of ice tangled into her hair, eyebrows thick with ice, her skin beginning to swell grotesquely under the beating wind. Breath slow, heart stumbling, she was in the region of what some think of as death. But she heard her name being called, Nyssa, by the one who did not give up searching. From a remote core in her mind's dark recess she heard, and still she hung between death and what is commonly called consciousness.

She thought she was in a dream. She thought she was lying in a bed and felt no cold, no pain. She rolled to her side and got her eyes open and distinguished with confusion the ribs of the boat. But it did not rock or sway or in any way move or smell like a boat. She lay staring and saw nothing from her right eye and only the boat's skeleton with her left. She roused herself up painfully on her elbows and fixed on a single idea, Do something.

She saw her coat frozen in the stern. She pulled at it and when it wouldn't move, she struggled up again and grasped the gunwhale and rolled herself over the edge of the boat, hoping the ice would hold and it did, and on her hands and knees she grimped her way to shore. Winter wind northwest, she thought ponderously and faced her cheek into it to keep from getting lost, fingers without feeling, feet without feeling.

Inside the rooms all silence. Donal could not play. He looked out over the gulf and wondered why she ran off like that and when she'd come back. There were no lights along the shore. He was thinking, I'll need to book a concert hall, get our pictures taken, print the programs. We'll need to set a date. When the storm's over. I believe it's subsiding.

The next morning he slipped along the shore and saw that the dory was gone. He put his head down against the pelting. Ice balls formed across his thick eyebrows. Drops fell along the hairs in his nose and froze, caked his chin and hair. He pulled up the collar on his coat and tried to turn his face from the battering wind but whatever direction he turned he could not escape it. Stinging ice crystals gashed at his cheeks like tiny pickaxes. A storm accepts no offerings. He tried to go over the repertoire in his mind. He walked back along the trail behind the house to take in some more firewood. He fell, cracking his wrist hard, and without a stick of kindling he turned and struggled toward home. He thought, If I wait she'll come back to me. I have to take care of things here. I don't smash fiddles and run out into storms. I can't just throw it all up like that. She'll come back—we always come back. We'll play.

When the small boys scavenging the shore after the ice storm found him, he was still alive, but they couldn't budge the tree that had cracked under the weight of its icy limbs and fallen and crushed his right leg. They put their ears to his lips and felt his breath. Some call it destiny, some call it fate. Donal lay trapped under that tree two nights and two days and thought about certain things. He knew that one act leads to another and that he could only act on what had happened before. In the judgement of others he had many choices, but he did not. He could only choose as he did, the web wrapped more and more tightly around him. Since the first time he heard her play there was no choice. And then she wouldn't play with him any more. And she left him. But all his meaning was now tied up with her and with playing with her. He believed that she had delivered him to himself and he was responsible to his own music. The difference was that his music was now their music, and yet he could not bring himself to go looking for her. And because of this, he might die or he might live, but if he lived it would only be by leaving his right leg pinned under a tree fallen randomly in an ice storm.

Peering up through her own icy hair Nyssa heard the familiar voice.

Girl, awake! Keening time.

What is this? said Nyssa, trying to raise her head.

The bony woman stood above her where she had struggled her way to the hole lined with blackberry earth. Frostbite ate her cheeks. Through the frozen glooming Nyssa saw Moll's legs with her single good eye. Moll sat with filthy socks over her hands, her thumbs poked through holes once made by toes. There was no smell in that cold.

Moll tugged at Nyssa's frozen feet and said, My feet are froze. Give us your boots.

Nyssa lay trying to move her fingers and Moll tore off her brocade boots.

What? moaned Nyssa.

Quiet, said Moll. Inside a woman is a wonder! She slapped her thigh.

Nyssa shifted, trying to get her other shoulder out of the ice. Looked for shelter for her naked feet. She could not tell whether she was looking into Moll's blank black eyes or the starless storm sky. Things were flat and she could see nothing from her right eye.

Everything happens between a woman's legs, Moll said. Out came my baby, nose curled forward in its little sack and couldn't breathe. My little mousebaby and I turned it over and counted its tiny arms and legs, one two three four. I dropped it into the sea and went back to the grub house and stared at a picture of a Venus with broken-off arms.

Moll whooped then, pulled in her arms and swung the empty sleeves to both sides like a pinwheel.

Look, girl, she cried, no arms to hold no baby. She craned her head to stare at the ice still falling from the sky. She said, Weak skin's my home. Your mother made this storm, and she won't stop it.

She sucked in her cheeks, pinched her lips like a fish, stared at Nyssa, her nose frostbitten. She said, The cracker berries gone. No one brings me a groaning cake. All the universe is between a woman's legs. Sure as worms.

She looked down on Nyssa's feet, naked without her boots. She took off Nyssa's sweater and pants and socks and hat. She squatted over the girl curled on her side, head tucked into her knees. She judged against her.

Nyssa heard Moll and did not move. She could not think what had made her set out as she had to come here. She was only sure that she might die if she could not rouse herself but each time she tried to rise she fell back. To venture to where there is no memory or conscience or any of the things by which human beings try to order what has no order is to go where life is forever altered by neither reason nor compassion. Nyssa was so frozen that she no longer knew if she was dying or dreaming or already hanging dead like a skinned rabbit from a meathook. She was divested of what she had been and did not yet know if she would become something other.

It is a condition of language to search for meaning in its most indistinct syllables. In the babble of the tiniest child. In the raving of the demented. Norea's talk grew more unravelled with each frozen day. She slept little. Dagmar paced down below. Rage murdered sleep. Dagmar tried to ignore her mother's talk. Yet perverse shards of truth escaped and sliced the air between them.

That last night Dagmar stoked the fire in Norea's room against the barren air and tucked her mother in with layers of quilts. Pinned under the comforters Norea listened to the tedious ice pinging on the window.

You make the tea too strong, said Norea, stiffly straightening her bird legs. This bedding's too heavy. And filthy. Did we spring clean? She looked at her daughter and was not sure who she was.

Outside, ice pelted the windows in a night beclamoured with noise.

Norea said, Shut the window. Don't you hear all that howling?

I don't hear anything.

When it stops you'll know you've been hearing it your whole life.

Dagmar shut the slats in the windows.

Not that much! said Norea. The cold hurts my eyes. My hips are terrible today. She sipped the tea, and said, Too strong. She shook her head. She recognized Dagmar for a moment and was soothed. She said contentedly, Do you remember how your father used to walk down to the sea with us to watch the seals?

I never met my father, said Dagmar.

Of course you did, said Norea, agitated.

Dagmar bit the insides of her cheeks to check her tongue. Her mother was confused. Her father. The seals. The bawn before she was born. A girl named Pippin. I'll get some more firewood, she said.

Don't walk away from me, called Norea. Then suddenly remembering something, she said, I dreamed about Nyssa.

Dagmar turned. What did you dream, Mother?

She replied, She was kneeling on the ice, a seal-meadow below the gaze at the top of the island. She'd come from as far as the puffins. She pulled herself over pumly rocks. She stood up and scuffed. Danced right here back on the island.

There's a dream, said Dagmar. Get a little rest, Mother. I'll go make you something to eat.

Norea said in her thin voice, Bring your father a bite too. I'll see you after I come back from the dory. Your tea's too strong. Make it weak.

She fell then into the relief of sleep. She dreamed words she had never heard. *Bamblys, piluinas, colinovis, kamovis.* She saw seals sea-silent, gazing unblinking from the brine at a poor barefooted creature. With ragged unpredictability her memory revealed and hid things again. Norea trembled as if on an open sea with no shore and no season, alive to the continuous torture of one question: who am I? Sometimes she knew where she came from and sometimes she did not. She sometimes knew Dagmar's tread coming in her room but sometimes she did not. She rarely knew if it was day or night, yet the habit of fierceness was alive in her still.

That night her feet twitched her out of bed and inched her across the floor. She felt for an old and ripped silk stocking in her drawer and took it to her worktable. She ran her hands over the surface, touching the things Nyssa had scavenged along the shore, pebbles and shells, dried seaweed and the sea's bones. She ripped open the foot of the stocking and tied the other end closed. She stuffed the driftwood and seaweed inside. With her stiff fingers she packed all of the things on the table into her stocking. She tied off the toe with her teeth and laid it down in front of the fireplace. She felt for the heavy iron tongs, picked them up, swung them over her head and down hard. Up arced the stocking into the air. It spilled out its guts of dried wood and weed like blood and caught fire on the rag mat on the floor. Shells and bones and pebbles clattered. Words chanted themselves through Norea's mouth. I don't touch the queen, or the queen touch me.

Then the old woman struggled back to bed through the chill room, pulled the heavy blankets over her and groaned old sounds to her aching joints and slept again until the smoke burned her throat. Who was that now in her room beating the floor with an old rug? She was thirsty and the smoke stung her eyes. She wanted to lift her heavy limbs but couldn't.

Dagmar finished putting out the fire and looked down at the restless shade in the bed. Her mother would burn the place down. She searched the room for embers, opened the window to blow out the smoke. The old woman's face was wan on her pillow, cheeks sunken over her empty gums, hair fine as a baby's. Dagmar tucked in the sides of her mother's blankets. She stood over the bed, watching the eyes moving under translucent veined lids, listened to her dry lips mumble, Dagmar.

Dagmar stroked her hair and her forehead and smoothed the deep creases between her eyebrows. She dabbed some water on a finger and dropped it on her mother's parched mouth. The old lips opened and the tongue moved out and forward like a newborn's trying to suck. Drop by drop, Dagmar helped Norea drink until the wandering tongue stopped its slow pulsing and the sleeping woman closed her mouth silent and still again, the skin around her temples gone slack. Dagmar leaned down tenderly and laid her cheek against Norea's. The touch burned Dagmar's skin like ice.

What is the effect of prolonged anguish on the mind? Norea swung her bird legs over the edge of the bed and stood on shaking claws. She put her yellow sun hat on her head against the sun in the cairn. Hand over hand along the cold wall she made her way down the narrow staircase and into the kitchen and out through the half door into the ice. She stopped breathing at the slap of cold and marvelled. Where was the little seal dancing in from her snowy raft on a fiddle tune? She was maddened by her drifty mind and she straightened her nightgown. She tapped along the path into the frozen bawn, sifting through chunks of ice for her stone markers and found her cairn with a relief known only to the blind. She made her way along the cairn's stones into the head and she sat down. The world was dying and Dagmar's grief was just begun. Where was Nyssa? A little song now. Perhaps the "Hauling Home" song, to make him laugh. But she was so warm. She had to get these clothes off. Blind alone. The silver thaw shining. Beyond, the ragged harbour, buckly ice and storm breakers.

From her hole in the gaze, Moll heard the voice that had long ago groaned through the bushes with her. The bony woman rose and left Nyssa's bluing body and walked through the dread cold.

Norea murmured without effect into the frozen air, Mow. Wretched dry sounds from cracked lips. She slipped into frozen delirium. She watched herself as if from outside, muttering, Open the door. She tried to move her toes, to lift her own parched and swollen tongue. She took off her slippers, her summer hat, nightgown, panties, bra and wedding ring. Six doors she passed through until finally she passed through the seventh door naked and bowed low. To her surprise, when she raised her eyes she could see again, but all she could see was Moll's blank black eyes. And she could hear now all the vibrations of the island. She could hear the sounds and sweet airs in the caves and in the trees. A thousand twangling instruments hummed in her ears from the sea and the wind. These things she'd felt all her life and now she heard them distinctly, too many for naming, all those long years of living her preparation for this. She could hear Nyssa turning over in Moll's hole, lined with blackberry earth, trying to rouse herself.

She felt a tear drop from each eye and roll down her cheeks onto the ice. Her tears warmed the ground and two mauve hepaticas sprang up. Then Moll judged against her and she died and the huddled birds in the cracking dawn fell silent on their frozen branches.

A frozen draft from the open half door woke Dagmar out of the still silence in the house. She wrapped herself up in her old green robe, toes shying from the floor. Her breath hung over the unlit Rayburn and the wooden countertops shone with an incongruous layer of frost. The powdered milk in the jug beside the sink was frozen; snow swirled around the table and chair legs through the open door. She stuck her cold feet into cold boots and stepped outside to follow faint traces of Norea's bare footprints toward the bawn. Unbidden tears froze on her cheeks. Through the layered darkness she traced the prints. Into the cairn. No lights anywhere in the black.

She saw the birdlike figure huddled near the rocks. Norea lay naked under the falling ice, one hand still clutching unwanted fabric. Her head was turned toward the sky and the stiff old fingers of her other hand clutched at the flat skin of her chest. She was huddled in a curl of bones and skin. She'd thrown up sickfroth that still clung frozen to her blue lips. Her head lay on an ice-covered rock, her yellow hat fallen off to the side, her feet already swollen into bruised mitts. Dagmar saw pearly blue blotches on her hairless buttocks all flattened under freezing ice. She tried to reach down and raise her up, to cover her up with her own old coat. Maybe she could be warmed. Dagmar lay down to press her own warmth against the cold body, but the old woman was stiff and frozen as Danny's jeans when she used to hang them out to dry on the line in winter. She'd take the pegs off them and pile them up like so many boards, cracking them in two and in two again and bringing them inside to thaw out. Dagmar lifted her dead mother up and carried her back to the house, her chiding and strange stories all silent now. She dragged her over the threshold of the kitchen door and longed for her to nag just one more time, Dagmar, keep going. You have so much more than I did.

She laid Norea on the kitchen table, went and found her mother's gardening dress and pulled her Irish boots out from under the bed. She dressed the stiff body, combed out the wetness from her hair and arranged her yellow hat the way she liked to wear it with a little tilt. No one left who remembered her father. Dagmar let her mother's hands fall to her sides and rest on the table, the way she'd stood all her life, plain and ready to move on. Then she stirred up a good fire and rested.

She was nodding off, her head on her arm on the table when she heard Colin's coin on the window, tap, tap, tap. Not tonight, she thought, forgetting the greenhouse was smashed. I won't go out with him, not tonight.

Dag, my love, said Colin, pushing into the kitchen.

Close the door. She froze tonight.

Who?

My mother.

He finally saw her in the gloom on the table. You can't leave her there.

I'm not having any coffin maker here tonight with his sorry-for-your-trouble-what's-the-length-of-the-corpse, she said. It'll wait till dawn. Have a drink.

She poured them both a whisky, set the bottle on the table near her mother's hand and drew up her chair.

Colin said, Dag, do you remember when we were young, when I tapped on your window the first time after you left me, she dumped a bucket of water on my head?

Colin was already beginning the tales and drinking that help the dead slip out of this world.

Dagmar's rage rekindled. The body was still thawing and him starting with his half-truths. She thought, I didn't leave. He drove me out and alone with a baby at that.

But she said, She was just nineteen years older than I am.

Colin reached for the bottle and nodded. Vexed with his drinking, Dagmar said, I want her back, Colin.

He leaned over her chair and tried to put his arms around her and said, The heart's dead are never buried.

But she pushed him away and said, Not her, Colin. Nyssa.

Over Norea's dead body, you're still at it! said Colin. Day gives way to night, Dag. You too must give way.

I won't. Stop telling me that. I won't! Norea dreamed Nyssa was back on the island. She said she saw it.

The harbour is iced in, said Colin. How could she be? I can't do a thing, Dag. How many times? It's not up to me.

Then who?

Colin stared as if seeing her once again for the first time and said, Stop the storm.

Dagmar took Norea's frozen hand and absently stroked it, playing with the tips of her fingers.

She said, I won't leave off.

Colin saw no point to meddling in the currents of this woman. His way was to abide, rise, fall, move around or sink under, like the sea. But Dagmar was a digger and a pruner.

She grew plants no one else could dare in that resisting soil and she prodded her children in the same way. When all the other root cellars were empty, hers had potatoes and carrots. She and Colin were different. It was not a difference of reason or passion but of different planes of being.

He never knew what Dagmar would do next and for the first time in their long life together he considered what might come of her rage. He looked down at the dirt he had taken absently from under Norea's hard nails and listened. He rubbed the tiny flecks between his thumb and forefinger.

Dagmar stared at his closed face and howled in an ecstasy of violent sorrow, Get out. Don't come back. Not tomorrow. Not ever.

Things change from one moment to the next. Colin got up and left Dagmar alone beside the corpse of her mother lying in her yellow hat and old boots on the kitchen table.

Dagmar wanted to stab him, strangle him, burn his sinews. She was judged for the crime of wanting her daughter. She breathed rage beyond breath, larynx, tongue, teeth, palate, lips. The old language was dead and her dead with it. She would stop the bend of time. She would not relent. The ice would fall.

After he slipped away Dagmar sat up and keened "The Mother's Grief," a song she'd learned from Norea:

By the time Colin came back in, Dagmar was gone. Not even a candle in the chill room. He looked at Norea's face, waxy and still, and said softly, There's no moon at all. I'll sit with you. I'll see you out of the world. I wonder what you hear there where you are. I wonder if you can see?

He held her hand, cold-bitten and old, in his thick fingers, then set it down and looked at his own hands. Dirt under his nails.

That night the people in the settlement could have wandered outside their rooms and felt the chill falling out of the air. They could have heard the ice cracking and beginning to melt. They could have looked up and watched the clouds disappearing across the sky. But they did not know the storm was over. They slept on, waiting and enduring.

One truth and the world split open.

Philosophers posit modes and means, construct a world of all things subject to limits beyond which they cannot rightly exist. For centuries men have grasped at such truths. But those Nolans of Millstone Nether subsisted heedless of such laws in the frolic wind, their souls spilling outside mode and mean, making babies from tears and ice from rage and melody from the monochord.

Dagmar found Nyssa crawling away from Moll's hole back toward the old farmhouse and she cried out and wrapped her daughter's arms around her neck and carried her on her back through the subsiding ice and took her through the half door, past her mother on the table, and into her own big bed. Her feet were naked and frozen. Her clothes had disappeared. Her body was bruised. But her lips still moved with a bit of breath. Dagmar called the women of the settlement and they wrapped Nyssa in warm blankets and bathed her fingers and toes in cool water. They fed her warm broth and untangled her hair. They restored her. Nyssa slept on and on without dreams. She opened her eyes and felt the movement around her and could still see only from her left eye. She sank back into sleep and the women put poultices on her right eye and willed her back whole and complete to them. On the morning of the third day she awoke wrapped in thick quilts, her feet and hands bundled in fishermen's mitts, a warm hat pulled down over her hair and ears. She shook her body out like an old net under the heavy blankets. Dagmar wiped her with clean cloths, pressed fresh warm poultices on her nose and fingers and toes and on the strange bruises over her body.

What has happened to her? thought Dagmar. She sat beside Nyssa, drinking in her face, imagining her green eyes moving behind their lids, rubbing over and over each toe and finger, examining her body as a newborn's for all signs of life. When she was tired, she let the others take over. She paced around the shivering, awakening bawn. She shook the apple trees. She rapped on the beehives, disturbing their dormant life. She wandered into the warming sheep sorrel, plucked up a dead leaf that lay cracked on the ground and ran her tongue on the lingering frost along its veins. The cold sun waned and she walked through the greenhouse rubble, lined up pots, picked up glass, returned to Nyssa.

Slowly Nyssa warmed and wakened. She was peeled naked and new. She stirred, took tiny spoonfuls of molasses tea and slept again. Dagmar stroked the crown on her daughter's forehead. The girl's eyes opened. She could see from both.

Nyssa looked at her mother, who had shrunk smaller while she was gone, and she raised her arms up to her and received as much aching love as she could stand. She knew that it was bottomless and forever and in the end passing as a fallen leaf.

What day is it? she asked.

The day after the night before, said Dagmar.

I almost froze, said Nyssa. I saw your writing on my picture tacked to a tree. Winds rocked the boat and I was afraid of crashing into the ice and sinking. There was a strange wake and I was drawn by it to the shore. I took shelter in Moll's hole when I could go no farther, but she tore off my boots. She left me for dead. I thought I was dead. I heard your voice calling me back.

Dagmar waited.

Nyssa said, Did he come after me?

Dagmar was silent and Nyssa judged Donal. She said, He would have let me die.

I could not sleep, said Dagmar. I imagined the most awful things. I tried to keep us from freezing and burning the house to the ground. Tell me what happened.

Where is Nana? said Nyssa.

Dagmar stroked her forehead and said, She didn't know where she was or who she was. She forgot that you were born and dreamed you were back. She said my father was in the house. She wandered out back and froze in her cairn.

Nyssa closed her eyes.

Dagmar said, When you went missing she helped me as if she were my own two hands. She carried pictures of you, asking the sailors, Will you help find this girl?

Nyssa waited.

Perhaps she was still searching for you or perhaps she was walking toward what she wanted. That was what she always did, soothed Dagmar. All things are possible.

Tears slipped from Nyssa's eyes.

Dagmar spoke from the place of wounding. I can see you now and touch you now, but you are lost to me forever.

Nyssa wanted to say, I will never leave you, but she could not.

All day, their minds at one, they tried to soothe each other.

Dagmar watched her mourning daughter and said with all the tenderness of an old woman for a young woman, There is always something left behind. That is the law. You have seen more than ever have I. You have so much more than I did. Make yourself better now. Make your decision.

From the sharpened edge, Nyssa spoke her wrath against him: He stays in his house and dreams of playing great concerts. Let him stay!

The storm was over and there were things to do. An old woman in a yellow straw hat on the kitchen table waiting to be buried.

The people of the settlement gathered with their fiddles and guitars outside Dagmar's house. They came through the door with a pine box and lifted Norea into it. They wrapped Nyssa in blankets and carried her outside where the earth was flooded with meltwater. A hundred fiddles and whistles and drums played the pine box out the door of the house where a young girl from Ireland had composed her life. The choir of fiddles drowned out the roar of the ocean. The whole island melted, running in long shining streams to the sea, the land damp, the air awash in water. The whine and scratch and tune of a hundred fiddles. They played "Barrel of Fiddles" and "Nana's Boots." They lowered the pine box into the ground, and Dagmar sang in the tongue she'd listened to her mother speak and had never spoken with her:

É ho `ro's 'na eheil air m'air.

And the other women joined with her singing,

'S mór an nockd a tha mi 'caoidh

Madeleine stepped out of the company, bent down and picked up a handful of the thin earth and took Nyssa's wounded frostbitten hand and held it and filled it. Then the young woman raised her arm high above her head as if she were brandishing a clay axe through the air and with one cocked eyebrow she let the earth fall on top of the pine box.

Dagmar dug with ardour into the thawing ground. She moved through the smashed greenhouse and cleaned and stacked up her broken pots. Trees were down everywhere. She wandered into the cairn and stroked two delicate hepaticas balanced on hairy stems, little patches of mauve in the cold.

She tended her daughter, split in two as if she were a chestnut broken open and both halves her. She watched and waited and wanted to hold her close, wrap her arms around her shoulders, run her hands through her red hair, devour her eyes. But as soon as she was up, the girl defied touch. She wandered away and would not sleep in the house. She took a few things to live down by the sea in an old fisherman's summer shack.

Dagmar, who could not yield to trouble, let her go. Now Dagmar was alone for the first time in all her long life.

As she piled branches and chopped trees for drying she looked around and thought, The understory will do very well in all this light and air. There will be plenty of sun coming through for new ferns and grasses. There are so many cavity trees now. The smaller, weaker creatures will flourish.

The old do not sleep soundly. She chopped harder and tried to wear herself out. In the evenings she wandered down to look at the sea. The ticklaces nested in the cliffs, small pearl-grey gulls soared in their great circles, rose off the water and whirled like gusts of snow driven by the wind. She remembered how she trailed after Norea as a child, learned to care for the strongest seedlings and kill the rest, how she made the clouds part and how she made things grow. Since the storm, the seedlings did not sprout roots under her fingers as they had once done and she wondered if a woman's powers are used up or passed on. Standing outside the fisherman's hut, she listened to Nyssa's chants and silence. She remembered the girl with all that kinked hair flying out of the apple tree at a summer bonfire and fiddling a reel for dancers. All that music.

One day Dagmar borrowed a fiddle for Nyssa and left it by the door of the fisherman's hut. The next evening she heard plinks and ringing notes. She heard the windy scraping of the bow played far from the bridge. She heard one clear, plain note. She listened to music that sees through, music played with the open ear. In one note all notes, overtones and harmonics ringing together, unperceived vibrations waiting to be heard. The mother listened and remained silent. Here in her daughter's music were all the sounds of the island. Here was the power that could grow seedlings and part clouds.

And when Dagmar stretched out that night in her old bed, her ears still ringing with her daughter's music, she thought about how much she had pared life down. To planting and sowing. To a lover and children and her mother. She had cut off anything that had asked her to be other than what she was. She had loved as best she could. Had it been enough? In her loneliness she still hoped for the tap, tap, tap, of a coin on the window. She admitted that if she heard it she would rise stiffer than before to walk outside in the dark to be with him. To be once again and once more with the watery one who lived not in her wisdom but in his own.

There is a time for the chatter of ice and a time for the passing of flesh. There is a time to test the mettle and a time for agon. There is a time to rest.

Nyssa was whirled and spun below and divested of what she had once been. Ice filled her veins and she was in the lowest deep, a lower deep. There she achieved the silence that portends a new tongue. She grew stronger and she walked the shore and the gaze. She picked up the little fiddle Dagmar had left by the door and found in it strange new sounds. When she tried to write the sounds, they did not seem to belong on a musical staff at all. And then one day two full seasons after the storm she wrote down a new tune and she heard inside and unbidden, fingertips brushing against her skin and the rhythm of a ground bass. That day she mourned fitfully, Gone is my love, my sweet love.

She walked along the shore to find Donal's sister. She called outside her door, Madeleine!

Madeleine was working on a large piece of plywood. She cut the board in half with two horizontal lines, one green and one blue. Above the green line, spaced evenly across the width of the board, were four trees. Under each tree was a different creature, a cow, a rabbit, a puffin and a deer. Below the blue line was a sea full of life, a whale and dolphins and seals and cod. She was painting a tiny border all around the picture woven through with creatures, birds at the top, animals on the sides, and fish along the bottom. She called her painting *The World* and wrote those words crudely in the border through the fish.

Nyssa knocked and she opened the door, her crabbed hands covered with paint.

Where is Donal? Nyssa asked.

Madeleine paused and said, I promised never to tell.

You know?

The woman nodded her head. Of course.

Will you help me find him? asked Nyssa.

The older woman stepped outside and said, He did not ask for what he found with you. He is much changed.

But he got it, answered Nyssa. Why does he think he can hide? All is the price of all.

He is afraid, said Madeleine.

His lips touched mine, said Nyssa. Our strings played together as one.

The older woman said, Would you like to see my picture?

She led Nyssa in to look at the large piece of plywood. Nyssa looked at Madeleine's familiar bright colours and light touch, flying things and swimming things. She asked, Why is he afraid?

Her eyes full of tears Madeleine answered, I cannot say. One can never know for another. I know only that I love him. I would do anything to end his suffering. I would give my life for him and share his fate.

Here was compassion.

Nyssa gazed at Madeleine's sea, the whale rising out of the water as if to kiss with its great tongue the cow. Against the sister's compassion the brittle bone of her judgement broke.

Find him, said Nyssa. Tell him his fate is not to run away.

And so it was that Donal, who now walked on a wooden leg, arrived back on the shore of Millstone Nether carrying his double bass.

The people of the island joked when they saw him heading for Nyssa's little house by the sea, It's in the blood of those Nolans. They knit their twine with holes in it. There'll be a party tonight.

They gathered at the pole house to see the girl with all that kinked hair and the man with the wooden leg touch horsehair to sheepgut. Together they played their "Passacaglia" and after, other things. Many times that night Donal's bull fiddle fell silent while Nyssa played her new sounds and new rhythms, unformed things that pleased no one but herself. When she was finished, Colin rose and said, Here's one I'm calling "The Ice Storm Reel." The young girls got up and danced.

The Millstone Nether people called for more and played together the old reels and jigs and strathspeys. They were happy to hear again the playing of Nyssa, who went her own way and Donal, who went with her, to hear the sounds those two alone could wring from fiddle and double bass. They did not care what would come of it. They were happy to play their old songs. They accepted it all in the same way as the sea caresses or destroys whatever falls upon its waves.

Near dawn when everyone was gone and Donal asleep, his wooden leg leaned against the wall, Nyssa heard Moll's kettle in the woods. She rose and followed the low moan up to the hole lined with blackberry earth.

She approached Moll warily. She listened to the bowl and to the dark one groaning her chant. When Moll fell silent and she laid down the bowl and bone, Nyssa asked, What bone is that?

You ask too many questions.

Is it the femur of a man?

Too much knowledge makes you old.

What man?

The one once called world mighty.

Nyssa said, Who were you before you came here?

Moll rose then to her full bony height, taller than any man on the island. The eyestone was tied in a pouch at her waist. Her blank black eyes reflected the light of Nyssa's gaze. Her fingers stretched toward the sky in an act of supplication and then she wrapped her long arms around her breasts to her back in solitary embrace. Her naked feet clenched the low browed rocks and she turned toward the seine-gallows by the sea. She said that she could not remember her former life, that she had been put in a state of perpetual mourning but did not know how or why. She said it was lost in the hold of a ship or perhaps beneath the sea. She said that what is lost must be found again because it mourns always under the surface but that she could find nothing and so she lived insatiable in the woods. She said that there was still more music to be played and that Nyssa might play it. She said that in former times a woman who went into the darkness was revered when she returned. She told how the people made processions and the women adorned their right sides with men's clothing and the men adorned their left sides with women's clothing and they poured dark and light beer for her. They played music for her. She said once again that music is a kind of practice for death. Then she was silent and she walked down toward the shore and disappeared into the dawn. Nyssa watched her go. There was more of her. Always more. There.

ACKNOWLEDGEMENTS

One of the oldest accounts of a woman's descent to the underworld is the Sumerian story of the goddess Inanna. The best translation of this that I know is *Inanna: Queen of Heaven and Earth* by Diane Wolkstein and Samuel Noah Kramer (Harper & Row, 1983). The story of Inanna's marriage to Dumuzi and her heroic encounter with Ereshkigal in the underworld was recorded in cuneiform by means of reed stylus on clay tablets that date to early in the second millennium. I have been much impressed by Inanna's vitality and daring. The first line of her descent story is *From the Great Above, she opened her ear to the Great Below*. In Sumerian the word for "ear" and the word for "wisdom" is the same.

Later, the Homeric Hymn to Demeter tells the story of Persephone, not striding freely into the underworld like her

Sumerian predecessor, but abducted by Hades, and of her grieving mother, Demeter, searching for her. My favourite translation of this story is *The Homeric Hymn to Demeter*, edited by Helene P. Foley (Princeton University Press, 1994).

The Dictionary of Newfoundland English, edited by G.M. Story, W.J. Kirwin and J.D.A. Widdowson (University of Toronto Press, 1982) has been invaluable. I have found traditional music and lyrics in Carmel O Boyle, *The Irish Woman's Songbook* (The Mercier Press, Cork and Dublin, 1986), *Traditional Folk Songs from Galway and Mayo*, collected and edited by Mrs. Costello, (The Talbot Press, Dublin, 1923) and *Old Irish Folk Music and Songs: A Collection of 842 Irish Airs and Songs Hitherto Unpublished*, by P.W Joyce (Longmans, Green, and Co., Dublin, 1909). I have listened to many contemporary artists working with traditional material. I am grateful to the Trinity Dance Company for their inspiring choreography and performances.

I am much indebted to Ann Southam for her discussions about composition with me, and to Joel Quarrington for his knowledgeable, sensitive and witty answers to questions about the double bass and the string repertoire. Thank you especially for the "Passacaglia." To Barbara Moon and to D.D. in New York, my thanks for incisive reading. Thanks to Alice Van Wart and to Cheryl Carter, Brian Mackey and Sandra Campbell for their insights through successive drafts. To Bruce Westwood and Hilary Stanley, many thanks for huge literary enthusiasm.

A special thank-you to my publisher and editor, Cynthia Good, and to Mary Adachi, for editing and discussions that have been transformative. There were moments radiant with synchronicity.

To Madeleine Echlin, Cynthia Lee, Adam and Ann Winterton, Leslie and Alan Nickell, I thank you each for your separate gifts of the love that "seeketh not itself to please, Nor for itself hath any care, But for another gives its ease. . ." To my husband, Ross, and to Olivia and Sara, I am daily grateful to you who live in the dailiness of it. I think Blake wrote, "Gratitude is heaven itself." Let this be so.